No **W9-AYM-898**

Harlequin
romance
by Anne Mather
comes to life
on the movie screen

starring
KEIR DULLEA · SUSAN PENHALIGON

Leopard
in the
Snow

Guest Stars
KENNETH MORE · BILLIE WHITELAW

featuring GORDON THOMSON as MICHAEL
and JEREMY KEMP as BOLT

Produced by JOHN QUESTED and CHRIS HARROP
Screenplay by ANNE MATHER and JILL HYEM
Directed by GERRY O'HARA

An Anglo-Canadian Co-Production

WELCOME
TO THE WONDERFUL WORLD
OF *Harlequin Romances*

Interesting, informative and entertaining,
each Harlequin Romance portrays an appealing
and original love story. With a varied array
of settings, we may lure you on an African safari,
to a quaint Welsh village, or an exotic riviera
location—anywhere and everywhere that adventurous
men and women fall in love.

As publishers of Harlequin Romances, we're
extremely proud of our books. Since 1949,
Harlequin Enterprises has built its publishing
reputation on the solid base of quality and
originality. Our stories are the most popular
paperback romances sold in North America; every
month, eight new titles are released and sold at
nearly every book-selling store in Canada and the
United States.

A free catalog listing all available Harlequin Romances
can be yours by writing to the

HARLEQUIN READER SERVICE,
(In the U.S.) M.P.O. Box 707, Niagara Falls, N.Y. 14302
(In Canada) Stratford, Ontario, Canada N5A 6W2

or use order coupon at back of book.

We sincerely hope you enjoy reading
this Harlequin Romance.

Yours truly,

THE PUBLISHERS
  Harlequin Romances

A Long Way to Go

by

UNA ROTHWELL

Harlequin Books

TORONTO • LONDON • NEW YORK • AMSTERDAM • SYDNEY

Original hardcover edition published in 1977
by Mills & Boon Limited

ISBN 0-373-02165-8

Harlequin edition published May 1978

CHAPTER ONE

'IT seems so final,' Nick muttered, 'I'm having second thoughts.'

Sue Howard pushed a strand of fair hair away from her piquant face and gazed at her brother appealingly.

'Mother was definite about it.'

She remembered that her mother had pleaded with her to take Nick to Australia and let him make a fresh start in life in new surroundings.

As they stood in the street outside the airline office Nick became stubborn and his lively blue eyes clouded. His pleasant mouth was set in petulant lines. He flung out a knobby arm in a wide gesture, his movements awkward, like those of a puppy.

'It's so damned final,' he repeated.

The London wind blew a stray piece of paper along the footpath and Sue urged her brother in the same direction.

'Oh, come on,' she encouraged, 'don't start a discussion here.'

'I'll buy you a coffee,' offered Nick.

'Let's go home. There's so much to do and little time left . . .'

Slight and slim, small-featured and big-eyed, Sue had to be the decisive one, and her will prevailed for the moment. Her wrists and ankles were fine-boned and she gave an impression of fragility, but there was strength in the set of her chin and her blue eyes were wide and candid.

They had both been away from home when their mother became ill. Sue was on the farm in Wales, caring for two children, and Nick in Scotland, in a remote area where he had been snowbound. He had not been in time to see her before she died.

Sue recalled her mother's anxious words.

'Dryden—We've been writing—He wants it. It's arranged, Sue,' she had muttered, in the half-delirium of pain and fever. 'The letter is in the desk. Find it—Go—Promise, Sue! Take Nick and go there——'

Sue switched her thoughts from sad memories and when they were in a bus, watched traffic flow by. The skies above the buildings were grey, but the boxes at the windows showed spring bulbs. Spring in London, she thought. It will be autumn in Australia. Nick will like the life there. I know that he longs to go but is hesitant now it's decided. He's seventeen, I can't force him . . .

He must go, her thoughts ran on, there is little choice. It will be best for him to start again and we will forget . . .

Mother forgave him, as usual. She was afraid of his weakness and must have felt that the life in the Outback with Uncle Dryden would be a challenge for him. She was so loving, so gentle. I had to be the strong one for her, and for Nick . . . I loved her . . . I love Nick . . . We must get away from the critical comments of friends. Australia will be sunny. We'll go to Uncle Dryden from Brisbane; we're sure to hear from him when we're there.

They went into the narrow house together and Nick flung his tailored overcoat into a chair. Sue waited and he turned to face her, flashing the sweet and charming smile which melted her gloom.

'Cheer up, Sue, for heaven's sake! We'll enjoy the trip, anyway.'

'It isn't a holiday,' she reminded him.

'I know. We'll work in Brisbane. Uncle Dryden may be a bore,' he added mischievously, 'the old boy must be worth a packet, though. He could be worth cultivating. Dad's half-brother—we could inherit.'

'Don't be revolting,' she reproved, half-laughing. 'We haven't met him. He may dislike us on sight.'

Nick, his mother's favourite, grinned impudently. 'The old chap isn't married. He owns this hunk of land and there's nobody else in the family, is there?'

'We may not like him either,' Sue said pensively. 'We must stick together in this, Nick. I promised Mother.'

He was momentarily subdued. 'I hadn't forgotten.'

'Then—don't forget!' She hated herself for sounding like a shrew and tempered the words with a smile before she admitted some of her fears.

'I've written to Uncle Dryden again and sent it off before I started arranging our affairs, but there's no reply. His letter to Mother was definite, though and he's expecting us. I feel we should wait in Brisbane until we hear further.'

Nick shrugged, not interested in the details. His young face was wistful as he looked round the bare room.

'Pictures, family things stored—nothing left but these few chairs and our suitcases. It's so final!'

She knew that he felt afraid and reluctant now, so she had to pretend to be undaunted, her tone was breezy. 'It's all settled! No looking back, Nick! A new life; Australia, here we come! We won't be unwelcome there, anyway. Mrs Morton has written to her sister in Brisbane——'

'Lois Morton, the arty one who owns the little gallery?'

'Yes. She's been kind and insisted on sending a letter off to her sister. I have the address——'

He echoed, 'Here we come. What's the name of Uncle Dryden's station?'

'It's hard to read the word. It's one of those strange native names, "Widera". He said that it means, "A long way".'

7

Nick brightened. 'I hope we see it. Do you think there'll be horses on Widera?'

Sue's ideas of the Outback were drawn from books and the occasional brief mention of their father's half-brother, who had gone to the faraway place as a young man. When they were children Sue and Nick had regarded him as a legendary figure; a story-book character, larger than life, riding a wide, brown land. He wore a wide-brimmed felt hat over deep-set blue eyes which scanned the distant horizon. Sue wondered if this mental picture was her imagination, or had she seen a photo long ago? In her mind he was lean, tall, with smooth, well-groomed hair and a reckless daredevil look, but now he was an old man, and her mother was dead.

'Show me the letter again,' commanded Nick.

'There were others, I suppose, but there was only one among her papers.'

She drew it out of her bag and the two heads, both fair, bent together to study the spidery writing.

'I know he hadn't written for years,' she murmured. 'I wonder why he waited until Mother was widowed before he invited us for a visit? You'd think he'd have asked us while Dad lived.'

'He might have been too engrossed in his affairs,' argued Nick. 'He's getting old and perhaps lonely. Mother must have replied to a letter from him when Dad died, and they picked up the threads.'

Sue pictured the man, silver-haired, seated in a canvas chair on a wide verandah overlooking hectares of green park-like grassland where cattle grazed.

'Yes, he could be lonely,' Nick continued. 'The old boy would be in his late sixties.'

'He's an appalling writer. The date is unreadable and I've missed words here and there——'

He read aloud.

'It's wonderful to think, Nora, that you'll come for a holiday and bring the young ones. There'll be room for the three of you. It's a good life and could lead to a future for the lad. There's plenty to do on the property. I called my land——' Nick glanced up. 'I can't decide if that word is Undina, or Widera. It could be either!'

'I think it's Widera,' Sue confirmed.

He read from the letter again. 'I called my land Widera. It's an aboriginal word meaning "A long way". It's far from the cities out here on the borders of Queensland and South Australia. Through the years I thought of you frequently, Nora, and of Bill. He was one of the best and we had a close relationship as boys. I regret the years that have passed when I could have been in touch with you both. Don't hold it against me, Nora. Come and see if you would enjoy life here.'

Nick folded the paper pensively. 'I'm dashed if I can struggle through the rest. Can you?'

'Bits here and there,' replied Sue.

'What a pity we didn't go while Mother was alive and well.'

'It's no use regretting now,' Sue said in a low voice. Her eyes were over-bright and she changed the topic quickly. 'He seems warm in the welcome he extends, and Mother spoke of him with affection.'

Carelessly Nick flung himself into the chair on top of his expensive overcoat and stretched his long legs.

'I might like the life, riding the range and catching broncos——'

'That's American!' Sue laughed. 'You'll have to learn the right phrases or you'll be another Pommy new chum!'

Nick grinned. 'You've been learning the Aussie words, it seems. We can ride, thanks to Megan and her ponies——'

'I didn't get much chance to get out on the hills this time. I was much too busy with the children and keeping the house going!' she reminded him. 'For goodness' sake don't announce that we can ride, not in that confident tone! They're *real* horsemen out there!'

'We'll both learn more.' He began to laugh. 'Riding the range——'

'Out on the run,' she corrected.

He got to his feet. 'Let's finish packing. Then tomorrow, off we go! To Queensland and, let's hope, to this place in the Outback—this Widera or Undina or whatever.' He put an arm through hers and drew her towards the stairs. 'Come on, let's get moving!'

'For Widera?' she questioned.

'Long way!' He laughed again. 'How right that is, Sue. It's a long way to go and a big step that we're taking, isn't it?'

As they went up the stairs she glanced back at the sparse furnishings. The room seemed bare and desolate without their personal things, the loved ornaments and pictures. There was no atmosphere of welcome and their surroundings had grown strange.

They were between two worlds now, and Sue felt trepidation at the thought of the future. She dared not weaken Nick by sharing her fears: they were committed now. They must go forward on the long journey to the distant place and trust that, in the end, it would not be too far to go.

Seated in the plane, Sue watched the stewardess escorting passengers to their seats and stowing hand luggage. Voices and movement created an atmosphere of excitement as departure time drew near. She had dreaded the moment of take-off, but they were airborne before she realised it. The routine of the flight began.

Later, during the night, curled sideways with her head pillowed, she could see Nick's reclining figure, relaxed and sprawling. He would not fret as she was doing, over what might lie ahead in Queensland.

They'd be wise to get jobs in Brisbane, she had been trained, though she hated office routine. She thought Uncle Dryden wouldn't be likely to meet them when they arrived, it would be a long trip for him. They must find out how to get to Widera and where it was exactly. A big country, and in the vastness they had to find his home. It was called Widera and it was 'on the borders'——

He'd write, of course, and direct them, she pondered. They had money from the sale of the house, but there were big debts and the balance dwindled fast ... Would it be expensive to travel to Widera? A train, perhaps? They must enquire when they arrived in the country. Nothing could be done until they were there.

Sue would send a telegram from Brisbane, but the town, the postal address, was hundreds of miles from where he lived; she recalled Mother mentioning that. So it might not reach Uncle Dryden for some time.

There might be a letter from him at the bank in Brisbane. She must stop fussing and relax as Nick was doing: it would work out. Uncle Dryden was Dad's half-brother and his letter to Mother was warm and welcoming. He would have them for a visit and they might be happy with him, and it would be good for Nick ...

Brisbane, the capital of Queensland.

Their decision was taken from them by a tall, pleasant woman with a square-chinned face. She was hatless and her short brown hair was greying. Her dress was smart, cool and comfortable.

She greeted the Howards casually as though she had

known them for years and they had come from across the street instead of half-way round the world.

'Hello, I'm Essie East. Lois wrote——'

Sue's finely-drawn brows rose in respect. 'How did you know us?'

'She's descriptive,' was the reply, and Sue wondered what Lois had told her sister.

'I'll let you cope with the luggage, Nick,' Mrs East said breezily. She stood and looked at them for a moment. Warmth touched her voice. 'My dears! You look so young!'

'We're not as juvenile as we appear,' Sue defended, smiling. 'I'm twenty-two and Nick is seventeen.'

'No sign of your uncle?' Mrs East glanced about at the crowded terminal.

'He lives in the Inland,' Sue said, 'on the borders of Queensland and South Australia. We didn't expect him to be here. We'll find our way to his home.'

The calm, unhurried voice was definite. 'You'll let me take you under my wing today, I hope? You'll need to rest and take stock.' She bore them off through the press of people. Sue heard her murmur something and it sounded like, 'A pair of babes in the wood', but when she spoke again, more loudly, she commented on the pleasant weather for April and that the summer in Brisbane had been a hot one.

'If this is autumn——! I think it's gorgeous!' Sue stood outside the building and tilted her face to the warmth of the brilliant sun. 'Blue sky and sunlight,' she cried in delight. 'Feel it, Nick!'

'I'm feeling it,' he said wryly, unbuttoning his jacket.

'You'll need some lighter clothes,' Mrs East said sympathetically. 'You'll swelter in those.'

12

She turned away from them and exclaimed suddenly, 'Well, I'm blessed! There's Rory!'

Sue saw a tanned face and the dark eyes of a tall, purposeful man who moved through the crowd lightly, as though his walk used only a portion of his strength. He was tall and looked over the heads of others as he drew near.

Mrs East added quickly, 'A nephew of mine did a series of photographs on his place. I've known him for years.'

Sue caught a glimpse of the man's palm as he held out his hand to Mrs East, and the skin was calloused and tough.

'This is Rory Stevens.'

They were introduced and there was a brief exchange of small talk. There was an anger in Rory Stevens that Sue sensed; he masked it and it was fascinating to watch the change his smile brought to the strong face, but it was for the older woman and not for her.

'You never change, Essie,' he said.

'I didn't realise you were in Brisbane, Rory. I hope you'll have time to call.'

'I'm going back to Yurla today, Essie,' he replied curtly, 'I have cattle to muster.'

She spoke reprovingly, with the ease of long friendship. 'You'd better have a good night's rest before setting out.'

'I expect to see Kent before long. Isn't he coming out to my corner in a few days?' The big man added, 'There's a bed for him at the homestead. The muster will be on and he could get some good pictures there.'

'That's what he hopes,' she agreed. 'He wants Outback stuff, pictures drenched with sunlight and with lots of action. Lois was enthusiastic about the ones he sent over to her.'

They dropped behind for a moment and Sue heard Mrs East's warm and friendly voice.

'What about Clare?'

13

'My arrangements have changed.'

'She was to arrive on the plane?'

'Yes. She'd written to me.'

'She must be out of her mind to turn you down, Rory.' Mrs East chuckled. 'Why, I'd set my cap at you myself if I were thirty years younger!'

He laughed in reply. 'And I'd grab you, Essie!' Then the anger crept into his voice again. 'The whole situation will be a lesson to me. I've been a fool. Forget it, Essie, it won't be mentioned again.' He changed the topic and his tone was indulgent. 'Are these two youngsters friends of yours?'

Mrs East nodded. 'Lois wrote me. They've just arrived, as you can see.'

'You're too kind to the lame ducks of this world, Essie.'

Sue stiffened and felt a flash of anger at the cutting remark. She heard him murmur 'Goodbye' and did not turn until he had moved away. Nick, busily lifting luggage into Mrs East's big American car, was unaware of the exchange.

Mrs East's home was built of timber, set high on stumps. There was an area beneath the verandah backed by battens and here green growth sprawled in profusion.

'Ferns! Look at them, Nick!' Sue exclaimed. 'Mrs East, what are those odd things like antlers?'

'Native ferns of the rain forests, staghorns and elkhorns.' Mrs East watched them indulgently and was amused to note that while Sue exclaimed about the tropical plants, Nick was absorbed in studying her car. She watched, unnoticed, as they stood below her in her garden. She waited quietly and let her thoughts ramble as she observed.

What an endearing sweetness there was in the girl's face, but determination when she was serious. Corn colour, that's what her hair was, corn ... pale and fine ... what a pet! she thought. I could hug her. Lois said she was good value!

14

The boy needed more strength in his face. Perhaps it would come . . .

'We need a cup of tea,' she said aloud. 'Kent, welcome to Brisbane!'

A young man rose from a big chair in the cool and comfortable room.

'I didn't hear you arrive, Aunt.'

He laughed easily and his face was strong and sensitive. He was tall and thin, as Nick was, but there was more maturity in his expression and more flesh on his bones.

'This is my nephew, Kent Woodley,' Mrs East motioned towards him and introduced the newcomers. 'What a pity you weren't home earlier, Kent. You could have come to the airport with me.'

Kent looked at Sue with interest. 'I'm sorry I missed it.'

Mrs East left them and went to the kitchen.

'Don't you work?' Nick asked tactlessly. 'I noticed most of the men were in offices and shops as we drove by.'

'Now and then,' Kent said with a grin, 'to get a stake behind me. I've given it away again, temporarily, to try my luck at something I've dreamed of.' They waited and he confided after a moment, 'Aunt Lois is organising an exhibition for me. I'm lucky to have her and her tie-up with the art world in London.'

'You're a painter?' Sue asked. She studied his face, whimsical and arresting.

Kent shook his head. 'I'd like to say grandly that I'm a photographer, but I've been working in an office and doing the photography on the side. I had a success with pictures I took on a property Outback. It belongs to a cobber of ours. He owns half of Australia,' he grinned and amended the statement, 'a fair slice of country, anyway! The photos, though—I sold some to a national magazine and some were shown by Lois as part of another show.' He paused and gazed out of the open French doors to the fern-draped verandah. 'If I could get some good stuff to have my own show, my name could be made! Are you a model?'

Sue laughed. 'Don't try that one!'

'You're slim, blonde,' he studied her, 'the far-away look in the eyes—delicate features and a lost-waif look——'

'I'm not lost,' she said lightly, 'I'm in your aunt's drawing-room.'

He studied her intently. 'It's a pity you aren't coming with me on the trip. You'd be a good foil to the harsh backgrounds. Where are you going?'

'Working here, perhaps, until we hear from an uncle on a station property,' she said briefly.

'Where is it?' he asked. 'I may have heard of it.'

'A place called Widera. It's near the border of South Australia in the interior.'

He shook his head. 'I've never heard of it.'

Nick interrupted, 'We haven't a clue where the old boy lives——'

Sue wished that her brother had not betrayed the situation so tactlessly, but Kent smiled and nodded.

'Away out there somewhere? You never know—you may come with me, after all!'

Nick rattled on about their trip and said it was the first time they were viewing 'the great continent down under', as he phrased it.

'I wish I'd seen your work when Mrs Morton showed it, Kent,' Sue said, 'but I was out of London.'

Kent shrugged in humorous regret. 'Some day I hope there'll be a pregnant hush when my name is mentioned and a voice will cry, "Not *the* Kent Woodley!"'

16

She was amused. 'Meanwhile you're waiting for that moment?'

'Not very patiently! Here's my life half over——'

It was the type of extravagance Nick used in his speech and she had to laugh. Mrs East wheeled a traymobile through the door and the young men got to their feet. 'Pass a cup to Sue, Kent.' Then she said in an aside, 'Rory was at the airport!'

Kent looked startled. 'The devil he was! I didn't know he was down.'

'Meeting Clare. It seems she had second thoughts. She didn't arrive.'

Kent grimaced. 'A good thing, I would say, but Rory wouldn't agree, perhaps.'

'He's expecting you at Yurla before long,' Mrs East told him.

'When I get a vehicle——' Kent muttered.

The conversation became general and Nick remarked that the businessmen in their cool shorts and long socks looked like schoolboys. They were interested in the timber houses set high on stilts to catch cooling air, the brick homes, tall units and prosperous shopping centres they had seen while Mrs East was driving them slowly through the traffic.

The conversation was friendly, warm and easy and, sipping the freshly brewed tea, Sue found her spirits rising. It will work out, she thought. We'll be happy in this country.

Kent looked at his aunt with a quirk to the dark eyebrows.

'These two are going out into the Interior. Why don't they come with me?'

'It could be hundreds of miles from where you're going,' Sue said, smiling. 'It's somewhere near the border of the

States, I believe. Broken Hill is the postal address, and that's in New South Wales, isn't it?'

'What's a bit of extra distance out there?' exclaimed Kent. 'Wait until you see it! And incidentally, here we don't say miles. We use kilometres.'

'Oh,' said Nick and Sue together, then Nick sat forward eagerly. 'That could be the answer, Sue. What a great idea!'

She shook her head regretfully. 'It depends on whether we hear from our uncle.'

'He's expecting us, Sue,' he protested.

'Not to walk in out of the blue,' she reproved him.

Kent looked disappointed. 'May I offer another suggestion? Just come on the safari with me. It will be invaluable experience for you both. If we pass near your Widera we can call in and say, "Hello, Uncle Whosis".'

They laughed.

'His name is Dryden Brooks,' Sue put in softly.

Kent did not appear to notice Sue's remark and Mrs East, turning from drawing a curtain across a window to subdue a shaft of sunlight which dazzled their eyes, demanded to know the reason for the laughter.

'I've planned it all,' her nephew said decidedly, 'they're coming on the trip with me. Share expenses and work—you see, Sue, I need a cook!'

'You could be sorry,' she protested.

Nick's excitement overflowed. 'That's the sort of experience I'd like to have. Oh, come on, Sue!'

Mrs East looked at her gravely and nodded. 'An excellent idea. I won't worry about Kent if he has company.'

Sue said in a small voice, 'There's lots to discuss yet. Perhaps tomorrow we could talk. We must find a hotel——'

Mrs East was shocked. 'Lois would never forgive me if

you went to a hotel! Your rooms are ready here. You two fellows bring the luggage up.'

Sue followed her to the well-appointed kitchen and saw a lively black and white bird flit nimbly from limb to limb in a spreading tree close to the windows. The garden sloped down to the brown waters of the river.

'We're imposing on your kindness,' she protested again.

Mrs East swept her doubts aside and refused to listen to her. 'My dear! Your mother was one of Lois's favourite people. I'm happy to have you!'

Kent appeared briefly to say that the luggage was placed in the bedrooms and that he and Nick would go and look at the second-hand cars in the sale yards. He took the keys of his aunt's car as she generously handed them to him and the two young men hurried out.

The activity made Sue feel weary suddenly and exhaustion swept over her in a wave. She had to bite back a yawn.

'There's the door bell,' Mrs East exclaimed. She walked through the gracious rooms and returned, smiling; Rory Stevens followed her to the kitchen.

'I didn't expect to see you again today, Rory. Sue has offered to wash up for me, so we'll talk here while I dry. You'll have dinner with us this evening?'

'I should like to, Essie, thank you, but I can't, I'm afraid. Is Kent here?'

'Didn't you see him drive out? You must have just missed him—he's going to look at second-hand cars. He needs a vehicle for the trip.'

'A car?' he said explosively. 'He should have a four-wheeled drive vehicle of some sort. The places Kent expects a car to go——!'

'Finances dictate, and he's too proud to allow me to help.'

19

Sue turned from the sink and her eyes met the big man's as he stood by the door. There was a spark that flashed between them and she felt uncomfortable in his presence. Was it the attraction of his dark masculinity—or an antagonism?

'There was a cable from Clare when I returned to my hotel,' Rory told Mrs East. 'She's on her way out by a later plane and won't arrive until tomorrow afternoon.'

Mrs East hesitated. Then she said carefully as she moved her capable hands, towelling a delicate cup, 'So she's coming after all. You must be—pleased.' Sue wondered at the effort behind the words, but Rory did not appear to notice the lack of warmth.

He said brusquely, 'I wonder if Kent could bring her out? It would be interesting for Clare. I'll have to fly out straight away. The cattle have to be mustered for the buyer earlier than I expected.'

'Sue and her brother are travelling with Kent, too,' Mrs East explained, opening a cupboard and stacking the china away, 'so there'll be another girl in the party.'

Rory's glance at Sue was sardonic. 'That will be an experience for you, Miss Howard. You're a city girl, I imagine?'

There was a hint of sarcasm in his tone and she bridled. 'Yes, I am, Mr Stevens. A Londoner.'

He raised dark brows and his mouth was wry. 'I hope you enjoy it.'

'I shall.' She was definite. The spark clashed between them again, but it was the electricity of a storm.

He said in the same dry tone, 'I'll see you at Yurla, then, Miss Howard. Kent will have a night or two there and I'll expect you, and your brother.'

'It will be unnecessary, thank you,' Sue said coldly. 'We'll camp out.'

20

What on earth was I saying? She had a momentary qualm. She hadn't the slightest idea what they'd be doing!

To her annoyance he laughed. Her temper rose as he said with amusement, 'I'm afraid the station hands would think it odd for you to camp outside the garden gate while Kent sleeps in the homestead. There are bedrooms to spare. You are Kent's guest, Miss Howard, so you will be mine.'

Mrs East said comfortably, 'Of course, Sue, bush hospitality, you know. That's settled, then.'

Sue said, between set lips, 'Thank you, Mr Stevens.'

She hoped Widera was on the track before they reached Yurla. They might not have to accept his invitation after all.

He turned to go and she heard his voice in calm, sure statements as Mrs East accompanied him to the door. It's decided, she thought irritably. Kent's permission isn't being sought about Clare, he's being told, as I was told!

She heard Rory say decisively to Mrs East, 'Tell Kent not to encourage them to go gallivanting into the Interior, Essie, they aren't the type. It's a hard area and they'll be nothing but a handicap to him.'

Sue was surprised at the stab of hurt the words gave her. Why should she care what he thought? It was obvious that he thought they were unfitted for the challenge of the country life.

When Kent and Nick returned Mrs East informed them of the new development. 'Rory called, Kent. You'll have Clare for company as far as Yurla.'

Kent's face darkened. 'How did that happen?'

'She's coming back to Australia after all. He asked if she could travel out with you.'

'Why couldn't he wait and meet her?' he demanded.

'He does have a property to run, Kent, and he's pressed for time.'

21

'He's in love with the girl. Why push her on to me? He knows I don't see eye to eye with her.'

His aunt laughed. 'Don't tell me, Kent, tell Rory, if you wish!'

He bit back the complaint and groaned. 'I'll have to do it. I owe him a lot for the help he's given me, I'll bear it for his sake!'

'That sounds very noble,' Mrs East teased.

Sue wakened to bright sunlight and saw the unfamiliar shrubs and flowering trees outside her window. Today was a new beginning! She would show Mrs East Uncle Dryden's letter and consult with her about the trip to the Inland. They need not go with Kent. He might be regretting his impetuous invitation. He would wish to be free to attend to his photography and not play nursemaid to two travellers who knew little of the country; he might, as Rory had stated, find them a handicap.

Rory Stevens! She felt angry colour stain her cheeks and found she was lying rigid, staring at the ceiling. Why did he grate on her so badly? She got up, bathed and dressed. There was a chill in the air, but she knew from her experience the day before that it was best not to be too warmly clad. Already the glorious sunshine promised a perfect day.

She tucked the letter into the pocket of her dress and wore a cardigan which she could remove later.

'I've sent the boys off,' Mrs East announced. 'I thought you needed the extra rest.'

'Sent? Where?' Sue asked blankly.

'Kent has to get a vehicle.' Mrs East laughed indulgently. 'His limited funds will decide what it is. I hope, for your sake, it isn't too horrible.'

22

'I meant to speak to you about that. There must be a train. We needn't bother Kent——'

'Train? My dear! You'll see for yourself the vast areas that aren't served by trains. A plane, yes, train, no. In any case, it's an unnecessary expense for you to fly. Kent rambles here and there and to go to your uncle's place will be no problem to him.'

Sue put her hand on the letter. 'You see, my unc——'

Mrs East paused, buttering toast. 'You must tell me about your uncle. You'll love the life, I know, and it will be good for your brother; build him up and fill him out.' She hesitated. 'I don't mean that to sound critical. You both need more sun.'

'The pink and white complexion?' Sue asked. 'I realised when I saw the men at the airport yesterday, and the girls——! Such lovely tanned skins. We looked as though we'd been wrapped in cotton wool! Neither of us has had a holiday in the sun for a long time.'

'You must take Australia a bit at a time, Sue. You're going to a hard and harsh environment.'

'Oh, I realise——' Sue began.

'Not altogether.'

When they had eaten Mrs East stacked the dishes in the sink and ran the hot water. Gaily-coloured parrots screeched and devoured honeyed bread set on a bird table outside. Sue leaned out of the windows, enchanted, her lips parted and her face alight.

'Isn't it lovely! Oh, you are so kind to have us here.'

Mrs East smiled at her and returned to her previous remark. 'Nobody can realise what it's like outback until they've seen it for themselves.'

The washing-up was over when Sue drew out the letter, but Mrs East was moving away.

'Let's go! I suggest that you leave most of your luggage

23

here and it can be sent on when you're settled.'

Sue followed and Mrs East thought aloud as she closed windows.

'Sleeping bags, one each. Groundsheets? You haven't any camping gear, have you, Sue?'

'No, but we——'

'You'll be camping. Oh, there are motels closer in, and comfortable ones. You'll be going to remote areas though. You'll take cream for your delicate skin, won't you? Come on, to town!'

Mrs East continued her monologue on the way downstairs to the car.

'Kent will see to the jerry cans for water and fuel. Portable gas stove—he's borrowing mine. Air mattresses for you and for Nick. Strong waterproof groundsheets. It *has* been known to rain at times!'

She opened the garage door and added, 'A groundsheet will keep the thorns and prickles out, and, believe me, everything that grows out there has a burr or prickle of some sort! Nature's protection, I suppose, in the hard country. And an extra blanket for warmth, Sue. I can lend you some of those things. Buy a space blanket, though.'

'A space blanket?' echoed Sue.

'They weigh almost nothing and are aluminium-coated. They keep the cold out and the warmth in! Some side research on space stuff, I believe.'

As they drove along she threw in another remark. 'Kent has a light nylon tent, but we don't bother with tents, usually.'

'You've done a lot of this?' Sue asked.

'I lived out there, my dear, camped out on the run with my husband when he was alive. Many times, under the stars——'

Sue's hesitation died. She was being offered the chance

24

of a wonderful trip. She must not spoil it with her qualms and fears.

'What about food?' she asked.

'Kent is a good camp cook, but I guess he'd like a hand now and then.'

'Over a campfire?' Sue's lips twisted. 'I've cooked on the farm where I was helping a friend, and cooked at home, but a campfire——'

'He'll have the portable gas cooker for areas where there isn't much wood.' Mrs East turned in to a big supermarket. 'Oh! Those steaks grilled over the coals!'

'I hope I can cope,' Sue confided.

'You'll cope, you're the sort. I can pick 'em! Did I bring a notebook to make a list?'

Sue followed Mrs East from one well-stocked department to another and they carried bulky parcels to the parked car. They visited Sue's bank in the city, but there was no letter from her uncle, and Mrs East remarked casually that there was no need to worry as bush mail runs were erratic.

Sue followed her. They moved briskly, these Australians. The girls and young men in the street seemed vital and full of energy, and Sue's doubts about her ability to face the challenges of the bush came back in full force.

She shook the weakness away. Nick was bound up in the adventure; he had gone off, without consulting her, to assist in the choice of a vehicle. The work of equipping them he had left to her in his usual uncaring manner.

Mrs East had chosen tinned foods and dried foods which took up little space. She had bought billy-cans for boiling water and cooking, and announced that she had light cutlery from her bush days that would serve their needs. And all the time the letter from Uncle Dryden lay in Sue's pocket, unread by Mrs East.

When they returned to the house Sue handed it to her at last, with a brief explanation.

Mrs East stood beside the stacked cartons on the kitchen table and read it slowly and with difficulty.

'Dryden Brooks is your uncle, your father's half-brother?' Her face was stiff and she hesitated, fingering the paper with unthinking movements. 'Dryden——'

'It's a family name,' Sue said quickly, 'Nick has it, too. He hates it and prefers his second name and the shortened version of it.'

Mrs East said carefully, 'Names such as those are often lost in the bush life. A redheaded man might be called Blue, or a fair man named Snowy.'

'I wouldn't know if my uncle had a nickname.'

Mrs East folded the letter and an instinct warned Sue that she intended to refuse information. The girl said quietly, 'If you know of our uncle you may be able to help me.'

'We all know *of* each other in the bush, Sue. Your uncle's property was hundreds of kilometres from ours, but we'd heard of him.'

Sue was blunt. 'Was he an old reprobate?'

'I know little of him, just the name.'

Sue felt that her lips were stiff. 'Mother was fond of him. She wanted Nick to come——'

The court case, she thought, I mustn't mention that.

Mrs East said, 'The name of the property isn't Widera, it's Undara.'

'Undara?'

Sue tried the sound of it, her face losing colour. As if it mattered how it was pronounced! Something was wrong. There was a feeling...

Mrs East said quietly, 'Rory can help you. You'll get a

26

better idea from him about things. You can see the country for yourself and understand——'

Understand? Sue was puzzled. Understand what?

Kent arrived back and broke into the awkwardness of the moment, followed by Nick.

'All set, Aunt? We'll have lunch and load up. Then we'll leave—we'll travel on into the dark and camp somewhere.'

The two newcomers were swept into activity and preparations, and while she helped sort groceries Sue faced the new problem. At last it seemed better to go ahead, as planned. She would see Rory Stevens at Yurla, and could make more enquiries there.

If things had gone wrong for us with Uncle Dryden, she pondered, Nick was going to be very disappointed. He had built it up in his mind, despite the fact that we know so little—Rory disliked them, it appeared, and he controlled Undara!

She followed the others out to the car. It was an early, and battered model of a large American car.

Mrs East shook her head. 'Oh, Kent!'

'It's as strong as the day it was made, Aunt,' he returned, 'I've bought extra tyres for sand travel and there's space for all the stuff we'll need.'

They carried the cartons of food, the camping gear, and equipment and stacked them on the lawn. She was appalled at the size of the heap.

'Well, let's tackle it!' Kent was in high spirits.

If we don't see Undara or Uncle Dryden, we'll have fun, Sue decided.

Kent was efficient. The spare tyres, jerry-cans of fuel and khaki kitbags of clothing were lashed to the roof rack while Nick lifted cartons and cases into the boot. The chaos he created caused Mrs East to order him to unload. With crisp

27

directions she arranged the goods neatly and, as she pointed out to Sue, in order of use.

'You won't need tinned foods at the beginning, so put them underneath and at the back of the boot. Keep the fresh food handy.'

Suddenly a taxi drew up, and a short dark-haired girl stepped out. Her slim legs and elegant shoes were their first glimpse of her. Her rounded face and pouting mouth were set and her greeting strained.

'What's this nonsense of Rory's? I expected him to meet me, and instead there was a message——' She tried to speak lightly.

'Some crisis at home,' Mrs East soothed.

The girl smoothed a thin dark brow and said bleakly, 'He spends too much time on that place.'

Kent surveyed her luggage while Sue and Nick were introduced. Her name was Clare Bedford and she was groomed, poised and glamorous.

'One small case, Clare,' Kent announced.

She said silkily, 'I need my things. Put them in.'

'I'll be camping,' he said, and gestured to the over-burdened car. 'Would you rather go by plane?'

'I'm flat broke.' She was frank.

'Then you'll be coming with me,' Kent said briskly. 'One suitcase!'

'Come and have a cup of tea,' Mrs East put in, 'and then change your clothes.'

Sue was amused when Kent went to the bedroom and she could hear his voice condemning or condoning various articles of clothing while the case was packed.

'There's far too much stuff in there now,' he announced when they came out for the cup of tea. 'You'll live in those jeans and shirt. You've put in a heavy jersey?'

'I don't intend to live in these,' Clare stared warmly. 'We'll change at night.'

'Where?' he demanded. 'For dinner by a waterhole? We shan't be staying at posh hotels, I'll warn you!'

CHAPTER TWO

CORAL trees were covered in flowers which resembled flame birds and fallen petals lay on the streets as their journey began. Nick and Kent were in the front seat and Sue and Clare, separated by a pile of blankets and warm clothing, were in the back.

They were beginning the trip to the Outback, to the strange new world. Sue was beginning to accept the fact that Undara might be a brief part of the trip, if they went there at all.

See the country for yourself, Mrs East had suggested. See for yourself and understand.

Understand what?

The first night they drove until late and Kent booked them into a motel. Clare and Sue shared a room, and the dark-haired girl flung back the covers on her bed and spoke with a tart accent in her voice.

'You'd think we could have had a civilised dinner! That scratch meal by the side of the road!'

'It was adequate, and Kent is trying to get as far out as he can. He said the distances are so immense——' Sue slid between the sheets, grateful that she had been able to have a hot shower.

'He's impossible!' Clare was decisive. 'He's wrapped up

in his work and in himself. I've seen him in action. You'll find out.'

It was barely daylight when Sue heard Kent call urgently, 'Get up, Sue. Wear that red parka thing and your black trousers. Hurry!'

Dazed with sleep, she dressed and hurried out. When they were seated in the car he drove down wide empty streets. Rays of early sunlight touched the tops of huge trees which bordered the footpaths. With care Kent chose a tree as his subject, checked the background with a grunt of satisfaction, and issued his orders.

'Stand over there and look up. More hair showing.'

'It's barely combed,' she protested.

She realised that she was the foil for the larger composition; the tree was the star of the picture and she gazed at it, fascinated.

'It's like a bottle designed for a giant, Kent! A magnificent bulgy bottle topped with green leaves.'

'That's what it is,' he grinned, 'a bottle tree. You'll see some strange trees out here, Sue.'

She answered absently, 'Your aunt told me that I have the name of our uncle's property wrong, Kent. She says it's Undara.'

He clicked the shutter. 'Where did you get the Widera bit?'

'From his awful writing!'

'Undara?' He looked up from the camera. 'Brandy Brooks's place?'

She stared. 'Is he addicted to drink?'

He said evasively, 'Sounds awful, doesn't it? But it's just a slang phrase.'

'Brandy Brooks.' A prickle of anxiety touched her. 'Is that what he is? A drunkard? That won't be a good influence for Nick!'

30

The sun grew stronger, but Kent had finished with photography for the time being. He put an arm about Sue's shoulders and drew her towards the car. 'Don't take too much notice of the stories,' he advised her.

'What stories?'

He grimaced. 'Heavens, I'm a blunderer! I didn't know that fellow was your uncle.'

'I told you. You weren't listening to me!' she accused.

Kent braced himself. 'He's dead, Sue.'

She echoed stupidly, 'Dead? How can he be? He wrote to my mother.'

So the letter had not been recent! She understood it now. Had there been other information which her mother, in her delirium, had not passed on to her?

She said slowly, 'I can't pretend grief, because I didn't know him, but I'm sorry—I'd like to have known him, though he may not have been what I imagined.' She hesitated, 'I'm not making sense, am I? Nick will be upset. He'd been looking forward to station life.'

'It's up to him to stand by you, Sue. Tell him.'

'Later,' she said evasively. She knew Nick. He could not bear to be crossed and he would blame her for what had gone wrong.

'You'll still go to Undara,' Kent said gently. 'I've plotted a track that leads that way—you'll see it. Anyway, talk it over with Rory when we're at Yurla.'

Her eyes widened. 'Rory? What has it to do with him?'

He stood beside the car door and watched her anxiously. 'Rory runs Undara now.'

'Runs it? How can he?'

'He does, that's all I know. He took me to Undara on my last trip. Your uncle was alive then.'

'Didn't you realise it was the name I mentioned? Dryden Brooks?'

31

'You said the property was called Widera,' he reminded her.

She returned to her questioning. 'Was Uncle Dryden running the place when you visited it?'

'I didn't see him, Sue. Rory said he didn't see visitors, so he didn't take me to the homestead. I took pictures of some donkeys at a bore, that's all.'

'Surely Rory wasn't interfering with my uncle's management of his property at that stage?' she enquired fiercely.

Kent closed the door and went to his own seat. He fiddled with the starter key absently, trying to find words to ease her worries.

'I don't know the story, Sue, so I can't tell you. You'll have to ask Rory.'

She sat rigidly beside Kent until the motel came in sight, and her face was tense. A niche at Undara had been a mirage which beckoned them at the journey's end; now the insubstantial dream had faded and they were told the place had passed into other hands. She realised that her mother's feverish ramblings had told only a portion of the story. It was just as well, Sue thought, that they had not come exclusively for Undara, and had no other plans. They would have to find work in Brisbane when they returned from this safari.

But what about Rory Stevens? How strange that he should control the run! She must see him and straighten out the situation there, for Nick was the male issue of the family. Might there be some profit for him? Should the property have come to him? How had Rory Stevens acquired it?

They must not be turned away from visiting their uncle's home and finding out what the set-up was, Sue thought. Surely we have the right——?

The ground was purpled by small pebbles among low

gidyea scrub and emu bush, and twin threads of telephone wires on steel posts were the only signs of civilisation.

Clare was in the front seat with Kent. She discussed his work with a show of interest and her light laugh could be heard occasionally.

In the back Nick slept, lulled by the swish of tyres and the purr of the motor, while Sue stared at the long slopes as the road wound ahead, kilometre after kilometre. Across the expanse of timber she saw a view of the far horizon, wide, expansive, blue deepening to mauve. It was alluring and mysterious.

In her heart there was a niggle of regret that her visit to the area must be a passing one. There was no permanent home for them here after all. Now she admitted, sadly, that she had dreamed dreams and made plans for the future. She had seen herself, helpful and happy, finding a warm relationship with her uncle. She had pictured Nick growing strong and self-reliant under the guidance of a mature man ...

'Whoa!' Kent shouted.

He stopped the car by the side of the road and reached for a camera, secure in a plastic bag within a special metal box, foam-padded against bumps.

'Emus! Come on, Clare. I'll get you in the photo.'

Vanity overrode Clare's reluctance. It led her to follow him, but she flinched as she picked her way through a tangle of harsh grasses and prickly bushes. The earth was soft and dusty.

'Oh, Kent! No——'

The red dust puffed up and over into her shoes, and she hesitated.

He smiled at her eagerly. 'Do you see the pale grass behind them? If I can get a shot of them stretched out in a

33

run against that background—off you go! Over on that side, and keep walking.'

It was some time before they returned and Clare was hot and dusty and her amiability had evaporated. She took off her shoes and beat the dust from them against the mudguard of the car.

'You oaf!' she snapped. 'I was mad to do as you asked!'

'You lost me the blasted shot! You've got to be patient.'

'Patient! It's a wonder you didn't want me to jump up and down!'

He nodded maddeningly. 'It would arrest their attention. They're inquisitive birds.'

Clare flung herself into the car. 'The sooner we get to Yurla the better! Stop fooling around or we'll never get there tonight.'

'No chance.' He was definite. 'There are too many things I want to have a shot at—the old stockyards at Bocka, for one. There's a broken down stone hut, too. It's about eighty kilometres off the track, if I can find it.'

'And if we get lost we'll roam in circles until the petrol runs out?' she asked sarcastically.

'I've never been lost yet,' he said blithely, 'but there's always a first time. I expect Rory will come looking for us in a week, if we haven't turned up.'

His teasing made her more nettled and she settled back in her seat in annoyance.

'What's going on?' Nick asked sleepily. 'Is there a town in sight?'

'There are no towns out here, mate,' Kent replied. 'There are a few small centres, a pub, a store and a few houses—we're in the middle of nowhere just now.'

'We certainly are!' Clare interposed.

'You don't mind the detour to the hut, do you, Sue?' Kent asked.

34

'Don't bother to consult me,' Clare said loftily.

'We came to see the country,' Nick stated firmly. 'Didn't we, Sue?'

Apart from her interest in the surroundings, Sue was glad of the delay. She was reluctant to hurry to Yurla. To confront Rory would need all her courage, and she had to tell Nick first that Uncle Dryden was dead and that Rory was in charge at Undara.

When they turned off to find the hut they drove through gates into vast paddocks where there were no tracks, and Sue found her admiration of Kent's bushcraft growing stronger. An occasional glance at the sun seemed to be all he needed as a guide to direction. He avoided low, broken fissures in eroded earth and fallen logs without deviating from his course to the north. The heavy car laboured and strained over the rough going.

A soft piled sand drift churned into a dark cloud behind them and the car swung and swerved as the wheels found no purchase on the talc-fine material. The spinning wheels bogged down.

'Everybody out!' Kent shouted cheerfully.

'I'm not pushing,' Clare stated flatly. 'If you will come into these stupid corners——'

'Out!'

She was firm. 'I'm not pushing!'

He leaned across and opened her door and his tone was level. 'You're part of the group, Clare. We all pull our weight on a trip such as this.'

The reasonable attitude angered her.

'The others can push. It wasn't my idea to travel with you.'

Sue and Nick stepped out and the silky-fine earth covered their shoes as they waited. The dust cloud rolled back and settled over them and over the car. Kent spoke lightly, but it sounded as though he meant it.

'I'll pull you out, Clare!'

Breathing heavily, she walked to the rear of the car and stationed herself there, but Sue and Nick knew that she made no effort to help in the ensuing minutes. They heaved and strained at the side of the heavy vehicle and the spinning tyres finally found a purchase and the car laboured forward.

Kent did not stop until he was on firm ground. When they looked back there was a pregnant silence for a moment: Clare had received the full impact of upflung dust and soil from the whirling wheels.

'Good grief!' Kent said softly.

It was unfortunate that he laughed.

Sue said quickly, 'I'll get you some water and the bowl, Clare.'

'I don't—want—it!' The girl's voice was harsh.

Kent looked concerned when he realised that she was upset, and his face was serious as he came to her side.

'I'm a hound to laugh, Clare. I'm sorry. You should see yourself——'

Sue filled a bowl with water from the jerry can. 'How awful for you! I have a flannel and soap somewhere——'

'My hair is filthy and my eyes are full of grit,' Clare said. 'I could kill you, Kent! You did it on purpose!'

He said uncomfortably, 'Of course I didn't. I'm sorry, Clare. It was an accident—you must realise that. I didn't know you'd gone to the rear. Don't you know that the earth is flung up?'

'How could I know?' she asked, her voice shaking.

'I'm sorry,' he said again.

'Sorry! What's the use of saying that?'

They left her and stood apart so that she could have

some privacy to clean up the dust and dirt. She washed, brushed her hair and shook and beat at her clothes. Sue caught a glimpse of her face as she leaned into the car to replace her toilet bag and wondered at the expression on it; closed, set and hard.

Kent had lifted his camera from the plastic bag when the dust died down and was brushing the lens carefully with a fine brush. His long fingers were deft and capable and his concentration was complete. With the basin of dirty water in her hand Clare stood and watched him.

Something in the silence warned him and he glanced up quickly. The bowl was poised and his camera was open and exposed in his hands.

For ten seconds the battle of wills went on, his forbidding glance holding her cold one.

Sue moved quickly and put out her hand. 'Let me empty it for you, Clare.'

The container tipped, tilted, as Clare tried to wrest it from her and throw it. The water cascaded over Sue's jeans and socks.

Clare burst out laughing. 'We seem to be either dirty or wet!'

'Do you want to change, Sue?' Kent asked.

Sue shook her head. 'I'm drying while I stand here. The evaporation is amazing.'

Clare walked round to her seat on the other side and nobody spoke for a few miles.

Sue felt shaken by the glimpse she had had of a deeper, darker stratum of the girl's nature. If she felt that she had been slighted or injured, she must have her revenge, it would seem.

The old hut was a roofless ruin with windowless gaps where sunlight poured through on to the red earth of the floor.

There were old bottles half-buried in drifted sand at the back of the house, but the summer suns and winter winds had scoured the earth to the hardness of concrete and there was no tree or shrub to soften the angular shadow of the building.

As she walked around it, and Kent studied sun and shadows for his picture, Sue felt a pebble move under her feet. It was pale, whitish, and she bent to pick it up.

It was the tiny head of a china doll; the blank eyes were filled with dirt and so was the small, perfectly curved mouth. She brushed it out with a gentle fingernail, and her breath caught in her throat. A child; here! She looked at the small dwelling with fresh eyes, picturing it with curtained windows and with a woman preparing a meal for a man coming home at the end of the day. The loneliness . . . the isolation . . .

For the first time the reality of the Outback touched her. It was not the background for a travel safari—it was a harshness, a beauty, a loneliness and a country which fought back against man.

She showed the small thing to Kent, on an outstretched palm. He touched it gently.

'It could be tough out here for youngsters before the days of the Flying Doctor, Sue. What a story the little relic could tell, eh?'

She slipped it into her pocket. 'I'll keep it. It will remind me that there were wonderful women out here in those pioneering days, Kent.'

'Where are we going now?' Nick shouted.

'To one of your towns, Nick,' Kent shouted back. 'You can have a prowl round there and see what a western centre is like!'

It was hours before they reached the isolated township which had grown up along each side of a wide, unsealed street. The desiccated cluster of wooden buildings was set in the vastness of space and diminished by the immensity of the open plains around it.

The small store absorbed their interest. There was an amazing variety of goods within the wooden walls.

'I might need some of these,' Nick observed, fingering the tough trousers for stockmen. He tried on a wide-brimmed felt hat, self-consciously, and posed for Sue against saddles, bridles and quart pots. 'How do I look, Sue?'

'Quite the part,' she said briefly, hiding a pang of pain. There would be no stockman's life for Nick now. How he had built on the dream, pretending he did not care ... She moved along to study the dress materials and groceries and heard Nick recite as he drifted from one crowded shelf to another, 'Bread, sweets, Christmas cards and decorations, paperback novels. Every blessed thing you could want!'

When the petrol had been pumped by hand for the car he could not be found. Clare had asked the hotel-keeper for the use of the bathroom, and had a shower, washed her hair and changed her clothes, taking as much time as she wished.

Kent pottered about the street, happy in the moment. He prowled, camera in hand, and found beauty in the metal lace of an old verandah and drama in stark buildings against the raw colours of the burnt paddocks. He posed Sue beside a signboard which carried names of far places and rolled the strange words off his tongue with enjoyment.

'You're just right, you know,' he confided as he peered into the viewfinder, 'you look sheltered and dainty, and the contrast against the inhospitable earth and empty country could be very striking.'

'I've a lot to learn about this country, Kent.' Then she added in a worried voice, 'Where on earth has Nick gone?'

'Search me. He can't be far away, can he? We'd see him for miles on the plain. You worry about him too much, Sue.'

'Do I?' She tried not to sound defensive.

'Come along.' He was cheerful when his work satisfied him. 'They'll come to the car when they're ready, both of them.'

Clare moved forward gracefully as they drew near, and Sue felt scruffy and untidy in contrast to her well-groomed cleanliness.

Nick did not appear until later. He slouched down the street with his shoulders hunched. He gave Sue one burning glance and without speaking, flopped into his seat. She sighed, knowing the signs. Nick was in what his mother had called 'one of his tantrums'.

Kent was oblivious of the atmosphere of tension. He drove on through the afternoon and Sue avoided a direct confrontation with Nick until they could be alone. For once he, too, was careful not to air his complaints publicly. Sue helped Kent prepare the dinner in the evening under the shelter of giant gum trees on a dry watercourse. He was deft in his use of packet soups. Potatoes were baked in the coals and there was fresh meat from the ice-box.

'Make the most of it,' he advised. 'It'll be tinned meat when we get further out.'

The meal was finished with fresh fruit and tinned cream and a good brew of coffee. Clare relaxed, lying against her roll of bedding, and yawned.

'We should be at Yurla tomorrow evening.'

Kent agreed. 'There'll be a good dinner there,' he said.

'Has Rory a housekeeper?' Sue asked.

'Of course,' Clare said loftily, 'Mrs Settler. Her husband was a stockman on Yurla and was killed in an accident falling off a horse.'

40

'You've been out there before?' Nick asked.

Clare nodded in the firelight. 'I met Rory when he was on holiday in Sydney.' She laughed mirthlessly. 'I was staying with my dear mother at that stage. For once I was in the right place at the right time.'

'Is your father still in England?' Kent questioned.

'No, he's in Spain. He has another wife. We didn't agree too well; not that my poppa spends too much thought on me, or what I like.'

So Clare was torn between divorced parents! Sue's ready compassion responded to a lost note under the harshness of the words. Clare seemed to sense that the atmosphere was sympathetic and spoke sweetly.

'I'm sorry I was such a pig today, everyone.'

'Forget it.' Kent was brief.

Nick responded absently and Sue realised that he was thinking his own dark thoughts. She went to her bag for a woollen cap to protect her head from the piercing wind; the temperature dropped rapidly when the sun went down and winter cold claimed the night.

Nick followed her and his voice was tense and low as he burst out dramatically, 'We might as well have stayed at home and forgotten about Australia!'

Sue stood straight and waited.

'I was talking to an old bushman in the township,' Nick went on. 'He said that Rory Stevens has taken over Undara.'

'Yes, I know,' Sue said calmly. 'Kent told me this morning.'

'What are we going to do?' he cried. 'The old boy was a waster, Sue. Mr Rory Stevens has his hands on the estate, evidently.'

'We'll look into it, Nick,' she said calmly, tucking strands of her hair under her cap. 'We can still make a good

41

life out here. We hadn't met Uncle Dryden, so we couldn't count on him——'

'I counted on him! He said there would be work for me.'

'We'll find jobs elsewhere and make a home, Nick. It's not the end.'

'It's all right for you, Sue, you're running after Kent—a penniless photographer! He'll be no use to you. When I think that we came so far for so little——' Nick broke off.

She was curt. 'You'll have to face the disappointment, Nick.'

He was bitter. 'I was looking forward to Undara. What about your Rory Stevens now? How did he get his greedy hands on the property? Tell me that! You don't know, do you? Well, I do!'

She broke in quickly, 'How did he get it? You've found out?'

'Uncle Dryden was murdered, that's what! That's what the old man said!' Nick mimicked the broad Australian accent in which his informant had spoken, and it was strange in his taut voice with his educated overtones.

'Killed 'im. Killed old Brandy. Killed 'im. You can't tell me it wasn't a killin'.'

Fallen gum leaves were thick underfoot and crackled as Sue moved. The acrid scent of burning leaves drifted in the smoke from the fire. She could see Kent, half asleep, sprawled beside the warmth, and Clare moved in the shadows beyond as she set out her bedding. Sue's scalp was cold and she could feel the individual hairs on her head springing and prickling against the confining wool of her cap. The cold was down her back and in her arms and legs and her face was stiff and unmanageable.

When she did not reply Nick said again, with a terrible

42

bitterness, 'That's the way you run things, Sue. I'll lead my own life from now on. I'll get a plane from Yurla—I believe they call at the airstrip there. We'll split our money. I'm going to the city, and you can run your life your way and leave me alone!'

'How could I know?' She managed to whisper.

'A great scene, isn't it?' he enquired. 'An old drunkard has been murdered and the man we're to visit is the killer, from the sound of it.'

'That isn't so, Nick. The old man you spoke to may have implied that Uncle Dryden was murdered, but not who——'

'Who got the place, then? Tell me that! We've seen the big homesteads on these properties as we've travelled out here. That means prosperity, doesn't it? Who got Uncle Dryden's place——? Tell me that!'

Nick turned and stamped into the darkness.

They were wakened at daylight by cockatoos which swept overhead, a cloud of white, crying raucously to each other. After breakfast the car was repacked and the four of them travelled through the day into country of treeless horizons and far blue flattened hills. They crossed a cattle grid occasionally or saw a large oil drum, opened at one end, set on its side to serve as a receptacle for mail and packages, and on these the names of properties were painted.

Towards evening a large mob of horses cantered over a rise; chestnuts, browns, bays and blacks. Their tails streamed in the wind and their manes tossed, gold-tinged by the sunset light. 'Yurla horses,' Kent stated briefly, braking automatically and reaching for the camera.

'Don't chase them now,' Clare pleaded. 'Be sensible, Kent, Rory will see that you get plenty of pictures of horses.'

43

He grunted something about the unusual light and hurried away to capture the spirit of freedom personified by the galloping horses.

Later they passed a set of cattle yards, solidly railed, and the snow of thousands of cockatoos in a dry gully beside a large windmill. Kent slowed and studied the scene intently, but did not stop, and Sue saw Clare breathe a sigh of relief.

The light was dying and it was growing late when they came in sight of Yurla; a large group of buildings with trees clustered about cottages and sheds. Nick's face was tight and he flashed Sue a hard glare as he sat forward. 'Prosperous, eh?'

Kent agreed cheerfully, 'Old Rory's a good manager.'

'You can say that again,' Nick retorted meaningfully.

They passed the entrance to an extremely large shed which housed machinery and Sue saw saddles and packsaddles and bridles hung neatly in another building. An aboriginal drove a rumbling, ungainly grader along the road ahead of them and waved as they passed.

In the homestead garden flowering gums and native wilgas stood among other native shrubs behind a stout fence and Sue saw sprinklers which flung droplets of water on green lawns.

Clare had her beauty-case on her knees and had been touching up her make-up as they drew near the house. When the car stopped she hastened to get out as Rory appeared under the big trees near the gate.

Sue, following, missed the moment of meeting, for she was butted unexpectedly on the arm by a large, extremely tame kangaroo which nuzzled her hopefully and looked up into her face. She was enchanted by the contact with the strange marsupial and her eyes were bright and luminous as she turned to face Rory. He dropped Clare's hands and spoke with extreme coolness.

'Miss Howard. Please come in.'

He nodded to Nick and murmured a greeting. The deliberate courtesy made Sue feel awkward. Nick began to fidget and she was afraid he would burst into wild accusations at any moment.

'Thank you, Mr Stevens,' she said hastily.

The unreadable eyes appraised her before he turned and, with long easy strides, he led them to his home.

He wore a blue shirt and riding twist trousers and a finely-plaited belt of kangaroo hide. His elastic-sided boots had a high polish. The thick, dark hair was combed smoothly and his brown face controlled.

'After you.' He gestured them forward at the entrance.

Kent was carrying his precious camera and talked of the trip. Nick was subdued temporarily and Sue was glad of it. She observed the thick stone walls of the wide-verandahed house with the name *Yurla* painted on the roof for air identification.

She glanced about covertly while Clare and Kent monopolised the conversation. I have a lot to discover about Yurla, she thought.

An eagle soared overhead into the blue flush of the sky where the horizon faded to pink and a pale lavender. Fairy martins darted through the cool of the evening and caught insects on the wing.

As dark cloud began to blur the twilight colours, Kent turned to Rory and spoke swiftly. 'Do you realise that Sue and Nick are relatives of Brandy's? Their father was his half-brother.'

'The only relatives,' Nick said sharply.

Sue had a confused impression of stillness and rigidity in the big man's figure as she stepped on to the cement-floored verandah among green potted plants. Rory's rugged face was half hidden in the gloom until he reached a work-hardened hand towards a switch. Only later did she recall that it was to her that he glanced as the light went on. She did not know if it was pity or derision she saw in his dark eyes.

There was a glowing log fire in the spacious room where they gathered after dinner, and conversation was lively, with Kent's laughing commentary on their trip. Clare laughed with him about the episode of the dust bath, determined to appear a 'good sport' and able to 'take it'. She sat on one end of a long sofa with one slim leg tucked beneath her and the strapped sandal flung on the green carpet, and her glance was possessive as she looked around at the plain white walls.

'The place is stark, Rory. No flowers or pictures. Basically it's good, but it needs a woman's touch,' she said teasingly.

'That's a fine stereo,' Nick put in critically.

'You sound surprised that we have civilised tastes in the Outback.' Rory's voice was level.

During the formality of dinner Nick had cut into Rory's comments several times, and his brash rudeness had made Sue ashamed of him. He was looking for trouble, but the older man had ignored his attempts to be provocative. Now he accepted an unspoken challenge; he turned from placing another piece of wood on the fire and faced Nick.

It was too much for the young man. Sue could see her brother's courage evaporate and the hot words of accusation falter. Here, in the comfort of the well-appointed room, with firelight on their faces, shaded electric lights above, and the beat of an unseen engine like a pulse in the distance, the drama of murder and dishonesty seemed ridiculous.

'It's a surprise,' Nick faltered lamely.

46

After a pause had lengthened Rory changed the subject with ease. He spoke to them all.

'You may care to see something of the real life we lead? I have to leave on a muster to the far end of the run tomorrow. I won't be able to entertain you at the homestead, I'm afraid. Should you wish to stay, any of you, there are plenty of books——'

'Whoa!' Kent interrupted. 'I'll be along! Why do you think I came? You'll come, Sue, surely? You're not tied to time with your arrangements?'

What arrangements? she wondered. Rory spoke formally.

'If you wish, Miss Howard.'

'I wouldn't miss it,' she said definitely. He thought he could evade their questioning by going away while they cooled their heels here!

'It will be experience for you, Nick,' Kent enthused.

Nick's attitude was cautious. Across the room his eyes met his sister's in a meaning glance. 'I'm coming along,' he said ungraciously.

Clare frowned. 'For heaven's sake! I'm not sitting around here by myself. How long will you be out, Rory?'

'Three or four days, a week, perhaps.'

She looked around at the shelter of the room and shrugged.

'I'd better get to know the place, I suppose. I may as well come too.' It was difficult for her to sound pleased. The prospect did not attract her, but she eased the lack of warmth in her words by stretching out a rounded arm towards Rory as he stood on the hearth. 'I may as well get to know my territory, Rory.'

Sue felt that they were intruding on what should have been an intimate moment. She got to her feet quickly. 'I'm very tired. If you'll excuse me——'

Kent yawned openly and ambled towards the door. 'Come on, Nick. We'll be up at daylight, so we'd better get some sleep.'

Sue was the last to leave the room after goodnights were said. As she glanced back she could see Clare, curled on the cushions, her body graceful and relaxed and her face tilted up as she watched Rory come towards her.

The door closed. One wonders how they'll fare, Sue thought ironically; she's used to getting her own way and he's so domineering. They'll have some battles!

Sue did not sleep well. She was physically tired from the long journey, but her mind was too active to let her rest. She was glad to see sun touch the curtains. As she drew them aside she studied the view of the garden from her window.

Where the hard-won lawns ended the paths were of concrete and each tree had a pit round the roots. There were signs of dampness in these and it was clear that water had been trickled into them during the night. The earth was hard and bare otherwise. She paid silent tribute to the effort which created a garden in the harsh area.

Later she walked around the verandah and saw Rory pass through a screen door ahead of her. Across the width of the back verandah was a separate building, complete in itself, containing several rooms. It was a chance to confront him while he was alone, and without Nick's tactless tongue to create awkwardness. She followed to the entrance and discovered that she was looking into the kitchen. A tall, angular young woman looked up from her work at a very large table.

Sue stammered, 'I'm sorry. I saw Mr Stevens——'

'The boss? He's gone through the back. Come in, won't

you? There's a pot of tea brewed, if you'd like an early one.'

Sue came in and the young woman's plain, good-natured face was interested. 'You'd be the English girl.'

'Yes.' Sue smiled. 'Sue Howard.'

'I'm Marj Settler, the housekeeper.'

'The cup of tea sounds very tempting, Mrs Settler.'

Sue noticed the spaciousness of the room, the width of gauzed windows, the generous cupboards and extremely large stove.

'Call me Marj. I'm widowed, my husband was killed falling off a horse when the twins were babies.'

'You have children to care for?' Sue enquired.

The woman nodded. 'The twins are five years old now, so it wasn't yesterday that Cec died. The Boss said that I had a job here as long as I need one.'

She placed a fat enamel teapot on the table and Sue filled a pottery mug with steaming liquid. She took a biscuit and stared at it motionless; the delicious aroma of the crunchy browned slice wafted to her nostrils and she found her eyes filling with foolish tears.

Suddenly everything became too much for her—weariness, disappointment and her repressed grief. Her face trembled and she felt her control slip from her.

Mrs Settler spoke sharply. 'Hey! Sit down! You're worn out, that's your trouble. Straight off the plane, they tell me——' She pushed a chair forward and Sue sank to it gratefully.

'My mother loved these biscuits,' she muttered, through a painful throat.

Kettle and saucepans were given a quick shove and the firebox opened for another piece of wood before the woman came back to the table, and by this time Sue had choked back the tears. 'She died a few weeks before we came out,' she said simply.

Marj Settler did not speak but sliced bread swiftly, her big hands capable and deft. 'Just drink your tea,' she said warmly after a while. 'It helps. Many a quart I've drunk in my time.'

They laughed together wryly and Sue ate the biscuit. It seemed right, somehow, to say farewell to what was gone for ever. It was eased by the warmth and homely comfort of the Yurla kitchen. For the first time she could think of her mother without sorrow.

She gave up the attempt to follow Rory and talk to him. She would have an opportunity later. As she came out on the verandah again Clare was walking to the bathroom. She was dainty in a beautiful soft blue dressing gown and her feet were thrust into velvet slippers. She stared at Sue disapprovingly and said in her sharp, clear voice, 'What on earth are you doing in there?'

'I had a cup of tea.'

Clare frowned. 'You shouldn't get intimate with the staff.' Sue heard the screen door snick shut behind her and hoped that Marj Settler had not heard the remark.

There were tender steaks for everyone, the usual breakfast on a cattle station; then swags were rolled on the cement floor of the verandah, blankets wrapped inside waterproof canvas groundsheets. A large truck backed up to a big gate, and Rory, Kent and Nick carried the equipment out to it. A large square tank of water was aboard, wooden food boxes were brought from the kitchen and the truck drove away. At an outbuilding Sue saw bales of hay for the horses lifted to the load.

Horses were brought from the yards and loaded into large horse floats. The vehicles drove beyond the buildings out of sight.

Kent drove his car to the gate, too, and emptied much of his load, stacking cartons on the verandah. Sue helped him store perishable foods in a freezing chamber near the pantry.

Nick came to stand near her after a while. 'Have you had a word with Rory?'

'I shall,' she promised.

'Have you noticed the size of the house? That freezer is the size of a room! The equipment on this place must have cost a wad of money. It's Uncle Dryden's money, probably!'

'Do be careful,' she begged. 'We have no proof of anything. Don't rush in with wild accusations, Nick. We'll speak to him sensibly.'

Rory came across to them, a wide-brimmed hat set rakishly on his strong dark hair. 'There'll be extra horses in the yards out at the Moonrise Bore if you would care to ride, Miss Howard.' He added dryly, 'I suppose we should be Sue and Rory at this stage.'

She said lightly, 'Why not?'

'Why not, indeed?' he said cryptically, and his expression was unreadable as he looked down at her.

Clare came towards them quickly, her tailored slacks neat on her slim hips and a multi-coloured blouse tucked in at her small waist. 'I remembered your instructions about a shady hat,' she told Rory, 'you scolded me the last time I was here. Remember?'

'Did I?' He seemed amused.

'When I was visiting with my darling mother.'

It jarred on Sue whenever she heard Clare refer to her mother, for it was obvious that the affectionate phrase was used in an ugly, twisted manner.

Rory did not appear to notice and swung away to shout directions to a man at the sheds. 'Right?' He waved a hand to Kent. 'Sue's going with you and Nick is travelling out in the utility with the saddles. Everyone set?'

He was accustomed to command, and before long they were on their way. As he followed the Land Rover Kent dropped back so that the dust cloud could abate ahead of him.

'How are you liking it, Sue?' he asked. It was the first time they had been alone and he took his hand off the wheel and gave her hand a quick squeeze.

She hesitated. 'It's early yet—I'm a raw beginner.'

He grinned. 'You'll fit in—I can tell. He's one of the best, Rory is! You'll like him, Sue.'

A long pause and she said carefully, 'I hope so.' She gestured ahead and changed the subject. 'How far are we to travel?'

'Search me,' he said amiably. 'I'll follow along and wait and see.'

'When can we go to Undara, Kent?'

'Oh, we'll go there,' he promised vaguely. 'Talk it over with Rory, Sue.'

'I shall,' she said quietly.

She was remembering the look of withdrawal on Mrs East's face, the frightening words the old man had used when telling Nick of their uncle's death.

'Killed 'im . . .'

Fear came over her again as though the harsh and brilliant sun had been obscured by a dark cloud.

Careful . . . be careful . . . this isn't as simple as it might appear.

The bore came in sight at last, sat on open plains where the windmill's steel wheel seemed incongruous as it pumped the artesian water to the surface. There were several huge galvanised iron tanks and a long line of cattle troughing protected by rails of bush timber. The earth about the troughs had been paved to protect it from the eroding cloven hooves.

Cockatoos and the pink and grey galahs wheeled and shrilled, disturbed by the movements of men and the horses in the set of yards nearby. A bough shed was set beyond the yards, the only shade. The girls waited there while the men caught their horses, saddled and rode away. The flies pestered them and it grew hot. When they were alone Clare did not keep up her pretence of amiability, and she swore as she brushed the crawling insects from her eyes. 'Why in heaven's name didn't I stay at the house?'

'Do you ride?' Sue asked.

'A bit.' She shrugged. 'I'm not keen on animals.'

'I'm not very good,' Sue admitted, 'not in the class of those stockmen! They're superb horsemen, aren't they?'

'It's their life. Why shouldn't they be?'

Sue shrugged. 'I couldn't help admiring them. The horses seem wild and half-broken.'

'Rory had better have a quieter one for me,' Clare yawned, 'if I'm awake when he's ready.'

'Did you ride when you were here on your previous visit?'

Clare brightened. 'No, indeed! It was a social occasion. It was Picnic Race time and Mother and I were invited to fly up for it. Talk about a gay time! They had horses from hundreds of kilometres around and people came in small planes, cars—slept in tents and on the verandahs—there were dances every night in the big shed—oh, it was super!'

'Does it happen often?' Sue tried to picture the gaiety and friendliness of it.

Clare snorted. 'Once a year! Can you imagine it? Once in twelve months!'

Sue said comfortingly, 'They work hard. I guess there

53

are a lot of very interesting things to do apart from the annual races——'

'There'd better be,' Clare said, and the sharp note was in her voice again as she stared at the baked claypan beyond the shelter of the bough shed. The steely sheen of the hard surface had begun to shimmer in the sun and waves of heat danced across the endless plain. Kent drove back from somewhere in the distance and came to join them.

'Whew!' He wiped his forehead with a handkerchief. 'It's warm out there. Is there a cool drink?'

Clare gestured lazily to the insulated container of cold water in the Land Rover. 'Help yourself.'

He drank thirstily. 'Come on, you two. You'll have a job to keep up with Rory when you're married, Clare.'

'I don't intend to try,' she said shortly, 'under these conditions!'

'You'll have to learn,' he teased. 'You'll have to be the little missus! I got some magnificent shots of the men catching their horses and riding off.'

'Don't you ever think of anything apart from that camera?' snapped Clare.

CHAPTER THREE

RORY had saddled horses for them and the two girls rode with him across the open country. Cattle were being gathered from distant gullies and hollows in low hills bordering the plain. Later lunch was eaten in the sparse shade of a few thin-leaved beefwood trees. The billy was boiled and sandwiches brought from the saddlebags. Some distance away the cattle lowed and moved restlessly, creating a dust cloud which gradually grew into a haze.

Rory came back to them in the early afternoon where they rode on the wing of the mob away from the worst of the dust.

'Kent is driving the Land Rover, Clare. Would you like to go on to the night camp? I'll let your horses go and they can be driven along with the cattle.'

She dismounted quickly and handed the reins to him.

He led the horse closer to Sue and looked up at her. 'Are you ready to call it a day?' he asked.

She wondered if the ride in the heat had been a test, in some way, and felt exasperated. She tried not to grimace as she slid to the ground; she would not let him know that she was stiff and sore.

He spoke dryly. 'I'm sure you've had enough. You'll be able to relax at the camp and ease the ache from your bones.'

As Kent halted with the Land Rover Sue managed, heroically, not to hobble towards it. Clare frowned as Rory began to unsaddle their mounts, his own horse standing by with the reins dropped. 'What a savage-looking brute that is!' she muttered.

Kent glanced towards the tall black stallion with a blaze of white on its nose. He said quickly, 'He can handle him.'

Sue studied the upstanding black and noted the wild, white-rimmed eyes and flaring nostrils, and the powerful quarters of the animal. 'He does look dangerous,' she commented. She noticed that Kent accelerated quickly and made no reply. It was as though he wished to change the subject for some reason. She took no notice of it, at the time.

The night camp was in the sandy dry bed of a wide creek where coolibahs and gum trees cast shade. It was some distance from another bore, windmill and yards. The cook had set up his kitchen there and tended his camp ovens and billy cans. An awning had been stretched between two of the large trees and the girls spent the rest of the afternoon there.

About four o'clock a utility truck speared across the flat terrain, visible for a long time in the distance but distorted by the heat haze. As it drew near the camp Sue saw that it was driven by a woman. She stepped out and spoke briefly to the cook, then glanced across at the awning as though she had referred to the presence of the two girls.

She was tall and wore men's trousers and shirt. Her hips were lean and the felt hat was worn low on her brow to keep off the sun. She walked with the same mincing gait as the horsemen in her high-heeled riding boots. From the pocket of her grey shirt she slid a packet of cigarettes and shook one out slowly, then she walked over and stopped a few feet from them. As her work-roughened hands slid the cover from a box of matches she looked at Clare.

'You're Miss Bedford. I saw you at the Picnic Races last time you were up.' Something that might have been a smile touched the tight lips briefly. 'Word has got around that you're here.'

Her glance at Sue was pointed and Clare said languidly, without moving from where she lay against blanket rolls, 'This is Sue Howard. Mrs Colter is the housekeeper from Undara.'

The woman nodded and lit her cigarette. Sue's eyes lit with warmth and pleasure and she got to her feet.

'I'm so pleased to meet you,' she cried impulsively. 'Dryden Brooks was my uncle—our uncle, I should say. My brother and I have come out from England to visit Undara.'

The woman did not look at her but let the freshly-lit cigarette fall to the ground where she crushed it with her heel as though it had become distasteful suddenly. 'My son works on the place,' she said abruptly.

She stood stiffly, waiting, her fingers stilled on the matchbox and the immense silence of the country enveloped them briefly. Knuckles showed pale on brown hands. Then, at last, the fingers moved and the box was slid into the shirt pocket. Her lips, innocent of cream or lipstick were tight when she spoke.

'The Boss never spoke of any young relatives.'

'My mother spoke of him,' Sue retorted, nettled, 'often.'

It seemed that Mrs Colter was about to speak quickly and passionately, but she bit the words back. Instead she said dryly, 'My ute is giving trouble, so I cut across here instead of going on to Yurla homestead. Sim can look at it tonight.'

'Your son?' Sue asked.

'Yes, my son.'

'Is he here?' Clare asked languidly.

'Helping with the muster,' Mrs Colter said shortly. She stood erect, apart, outside the shade of the awning.

'Won't you sit down?' Sue asked. 'We found the bed-rolls comfortable——'

'No, thanks.' Mrs Colter turned and walked back to the utility, and the snap of the closing door was a punctuation mark to the conversation. Sue longed to go to her and speak of her uncle, but the woman was so unyielding and aloof that she did not dare.

'Odd type,' Clare said acidly. 'Look at her, sitting up in the cabin, staring straight ahead. She's probably a bit batty from living in the bush.'

Sue watched uneasily. It had been obvious that it was her own presence which caused the awkwardness; Mrs Colter had seemed friendly to Clare as the future wife of a neighbour. Or as the future wife of the man who controlled Undara.

Was it because Clare was to be the Boss's wife, Mrs Stevens of Yurla, that she had been treated with respect?

57

There was no servile attitude in Mrs Colter, however. She was independent and proud and seemed to be accustomed to making her own decisions. When she had referred to 'the Boss' she had meant Dryden Brooks. My uncle, Sue thought, and I haven't the courage to walk across that strip of baked earth to her and speak of him in a natural manner. I feel she might wind up the window as I approached!

Before the men returned Sue found her toilet bag and towel, took a container of water and walked upstream to a sheltered nook behind tree trunks and high earth banks. Here she washed, brushed her hair and returned feeling refreshed.

Clare moaned, 'Oh, how primitive! Not even a proper bath!'

It was growing cooler and the sun coloured the western sky in a lavish display of gold and red. Sue stood enthralled, hardly aware of Clare's muttered comments or of her going away to change for the evening.

Birds flew low, their wings black against the sky. From the campfire an appetising smell drifted on the still air, and she strolled over, dismissing Clare's jibe about talking to the staff. The cook was an elderly man, grey-headed, and pleased that she was interested in the results he achieved with his bush equipment.

When Clare came back to the awning she scowled towards Sue and when they were together again she was terse. 'You're a great one for hobnobbing with the hands,' she observed.

'Why not?' Sue was curt. 'We're all people, aren't we?'

Clare shrugged. 'You go in for the common touch, evidently.'

Sue had to hold in her quick temper. She walked away in case she made a furious reply. It would not do to quarrel with Clare! She was Rory's guest, for the time, whether she was welcome or not!

The men had yarded the cattle and they fed their horses before they came to the campfire for their meal. They were fit, flat-stomached and tough; wide hats were thrust back from their foreheads now that the cool of evening approached. The high-heeled, elastic-sided boots gave them a pigeon-toed gait. They wore wide leather belts low on lean hips and the tight-fitting, narrow-legged trousers added extra leanness to their muscular legs.

Nick, saddle-sore and red-eyed, had ridden with the men all day, but whether he had been a help or hindrance Sue did not know.

He brought his plate of food and sat beside her. 'God, I'm tired! Every bone in my body is broken.'

His usual exaggeration amused her, but she had to laugh in rueful agreement. 'I hope to feel better tomorrow.'

'The food is damned good, Sue. Rory does the men well, doesn't he?'

'It keeps them happy, I suppose. They lead very hard lives.'

Nick scowled. 'I'm going to have a go at that blasted Rory tonight, Sue. I haven't been able to get near him all day——'

'I'm here if you want me,' a voice said behind them.

He had washed, as the men had done, at the bore and his hair was still wet. He seemed very tall as he stood above them.

Sue swung to face him. Seated at his feet she was at a disadvantage before she began. 'We came out to see our uncle,' she began lamely.

Nick stood up. She could see that he felt discomfited too, balancing his plate and not being able to choose the moment when he would have made his attack.

59

'Dryden Brooks,' he put in, trying to regain his self-possession.

Rory said quietly, 'He died three months ago. Kent tells me you hadn't heard of his death.'

For a moment he watched her again and she had the feeling that he was sorry for her, but when he spoke it was not in sympathy but in censure. 'What utter folly,' he said roughly, 'to come out here without writing first!'

At his caustic tone Sue grew defensive. 'Of course we wrote!'

'We didn't imagine that he wouldn't be here.' Nick sounded as though his assurance was seeping away.

It was growing darker and a pressure gas lantern had been lit. Sue saw Kent hand Clare a mug of coffee and crouch on his heels, as the stockmen did, while his intent gaze studied the men's faces in the light.

Isolated from the group, and from the fire, Sue felt the chill of night touch her skin. Her fork clattered on her plate as she got to her feet.

Rory's face was a dark blur, craggy line of cheek and brow black against the lantern glow, mouth firm and grim in outline. He said flatly, 'There's nothing at Undara for you, for either of you. You would be better to return home. You're welcome to stay at Yurla until it can be arranged.'

Nick's temper flared. 'How generous! You've got Undara, they tell me. You've taken over the place! And now you have the cheek to offer us hospitality!'

'Do you question my right to Undara?' There was an edge to Rory's voice.

Nick's temper drove him to folly. 'By God I do! Look at the money tied up here—look at it! I'm a blood relative of Dryden Brooks. You're not! How did you come into possession of his land—and how did he die? Tell me that?'

Rory's body was very still and Sue saw his head turn

slowly so that the light fell on the set, angry planes of his cheek. 'Do you share your brother's wild questions, Sue?'

He sounded cold and disinterested and it stiffened her resolution, but before she could speak Nick rushed into accusation again.

'We heard—on the way here we heard that the circumstances of his death were suspicious.'

The icy voice cut in, 'Are you accusing me of killing your uncle for gain?'

Nick, belatedly aware of the dangerous area into which he had ventured, withdrew swiftly. 'I heard—I heard that it was odd—that he'd been killed——'

'There is talk, I believe.' The calm voice dismissed it. 'No proof, but—talk. Bushmen are as superstitious as sailors and as fond of gossip.'

'Surely the police——?' Sue said uncertainly.

'It was an accident.'

'But the ones who were there?' she protested faintly. 'Weren't they asked?'

'I was there,' he said with furious patience. 'The overseer was there and his mother, Mrs Colter. Also an elderly man, Frank Waters, who works on the place. *We* were there. You've met Mrs Colter, her son is the tall man standing beside her now. The big man beside the fire is Frank. He was Dryden's mate on many bush trips.' He added warningly, 'I advise you not to rush in with your ridiculous prying, either of you. You know nobody out here and are on strange territory. Be careful!'

Twigs crackled under his feet as he left them. Sue spoke under her breath, appalled. 'Oh, Nick! How could you? You have no evidence of anything wrong with Uncle's death and you've come out with a point-blank——'

He was stubborn. 'None of them will talk, Sue. I've ridden beside the men and tried to talk to them about

61

Undara and it's just as if you mention a dirty word. They find an excuse to canter off and leave—it's a damned conspiracy of silence.'

Sue groaned inwardly, picturing Nick's lack of finesse and the brashness with which he would approach the subject.

'For goodness' sake, stop questioning!' she exploded. 'We'll go to Undara ourselves. It's the only thing to do.'

'How?' he argued. 'We're stuck here at the mercy of that Rory!'

She did not like the sinister ring of the phrase. 'Kent will take us,' she said.

'You won't get him away until he has the shots he wants. Clare's right, he's a nut! A bullock nearly gored him today. He stood his ground until the last second and the red-eyed beast was almost on top of him. If one of the ringers hadn't cut in and headed the brute off, Kent would have been minced up. All he said was, "What a beaut angle!"'

Sue laughed. 'That's dedication!'

The ringers withdrew as the talk at the fire quietened, and they camped further downstream out of sight. Mrs Colter and her son kept to themselves, Sue noticed, and left the fire as soon as they had eaten. A small brilliant light burned where the man worked at the motor of his mother's utility. Later, the engine could be heard as it was tested several times.

Clare sat on her bedroll near Rory by the fire and Sue and Nick kept away from them. Sue felt she could not face him since Nick's outburst, and her embarrassment at having to stay at Yurla deepened.

They were prisoners of circumstances now. Kent, as Nick bitterly averred, would not want to leave at this juncture when the subjects he wished to portray were to hand, and it would be unfair to demand it. Nor could they expect Rory to take them to the homestead. He was in charge here, and the management of the muster was his concern.

In an odd way they were prisoners. No doubt a man could be spared to drive them to the airstrip, but it would achieve nothing. They would not have been to Undara, which was the object of their visit. The mystery of Undara would remain hidden.

I won't go away, Sue decided. We'll have to stick it out, however awkward it may be.

She heard the sound of cockatoos as they squabbled and shrilled, settling for the night in distant trees. It had an alien, lonely sound and she sighed. It was far from London and the safety of the life which they had known; here everything was unfamiliar and strange to them. She wished she had not been drawn into a situation where she felt tense and afraid.

The fire blazed up suddenly and painted the trees with dancing light. Sue had heard no talk between Clare and Rory. They did not appear to be conversing. Clare seemed drowsy, leaning against his knee, her dark head drooped. Kent had followed the men, camera and flashlight in hand.

Rory glanced at the luminous dial of his watch and eased Clare up lightly. 'Come on. We have another early morning ahead.'

It was not the situation for romance. They were to have little chance of being alone, Sue reflected. A bit hard on Clare, after coming so far...

She had to admire the control which made Rory's voice normal and easy when he spoke again, as though there had been no hot words between them. 'I'll spread your bedroll out, Sue. It needs practice to make it comfortable.'

He was quick and economical in his movements, brushing aside small stones and broken sticks before he spread her bedding and Clare's. Nick watched and flung his own down not far from his sister's and kept his back to the older man as he worked.

Sue was on her knees when Mrs Colter walked into the camp again. She had a plaited stockwhip looped over her arm as though it were the most natural thing to carry about at that hour, as she consulted Rory about something. He bent his head to listen for, tall as she was, he was taller. Taking things from her bag and stealing glances at them unobserved, Sue saw how thin the woman was. That was why the men's clothing seemed right on her; she had the same look of endurance and whipcord toughness. The country fitted her and she fitted the country.

The light dimmed as the fire died to a bed of coals and Clare, with calm confidence that her need justified her action, walked away with the lantern and went up to the secluded corner of the creek to change into her nightclothes. After a while Sue followed with her torch to light her way. She heard Nick hiss her name behind her in the dark.

'What are we to do?' he demanded.

She made her tone soothing. 'Nothing. Sit it out for now and bide our time. Goodnight, Nick.'

She pictured him standing in the shadows, taut, highly-strung and spoiled. She heard in his voice the leashed annoyance of his longing for action.

'Just what you *would* say!' he fumed.

She followed the light and Clare, struggling to find places to lay her clothes where they would not pick up burrs, was derisive. 'It's no picnic, I can assure you! I'll insist on a tent next time. You should see the dust on my nightie! You're lucky you have a track suit.'

'So much easier for crawling in and out of a sleeping bag,' Sue agreed. This had been Mrs East's suggestion, and Sue blessed her for it and for her help and knowledge.

The two girls returned together and Sue glanced across at Nick. He had moved his bedding and was closer than before. She called a general 'Goodnight' and snuggled into her bag as Kent returned. He replied cheerfully.

The large gum tree was directly overhead. She had not realised she was so close to the trunk of the tree when she had sorted out her nightwear. Had Nick moved everything? Why should he?

Clare stood by the fire, stretching luxuriously, her warm dressing gown buttoned to her chin. Rory made some comment and they laughed. He dragged heavier logs together over the fire and it began to crackle again, providing warmth for the sleepers.

Though we're too far away to benefit, Sue decided wryly. Well, I suppose Rory doesn't want us too close.

The tree creaked overhead and the wind strengthened. It sighed in the leaves like the sound of the ancient sea which once had covered the land. Brilliant stars flashed in the night sky and an owl called monotonously. The moon rose, a great golden orb in the east. Overcome by tiredness, the open air and the long day, Sue slept.

She wakened later, feeling some hard object beneath her back, and turned restlessly. Her right hand slid up her left wrist and she woke in dismay.

Mother's watch! She recalled that when she and Clare had washed earlier in the afternoon, she had hung her clothing on outthrust pieces of limb in an endeavour to keep them from prickles and sand. She had laid the watch on a small flat surface on the bole of a tree, and it was there now. She dared not leave it until dawn. What if the glitter attracted a bird which would fly off with it?

She unzipped the sleeping bag and slid out of it, felt for her torch and shook her shoes briskly, as Kent had warned her to do, in case some creeping insect had sought refuge there. She eased them on and found her way along the creek bed in the patches of moonlight among the trees, and flashed the torch towards the trunk of the great tree which had provided privacy for them. Metal glittered in the light and she reached for it thankfully.

How careless of me! I must keep my wits about me and not let worry undermine common sense, she told herself sternly, and turned to go back to the camp.

Dried leaves crackled as somebody moved ahead of her. She stopped in alarm but heard nothing else, so she flashed the beam of light among the trees to disperse the darkness of the shadows. Perhaps it was an animal? She was nervous, not knowing what perils the night could hold. There were no wild beasts in Australia—were there?

She tried not to hurry, or let her panic rise. She had gone a few more steps when there was a sharp cracking sound and a rending of timber.

Clare screamed in sudden terror.

Sue could hear Nick's voice, high-pitched, shouting something, and Rory's deeper tones spoke quickly in command. The light blazed suddenly as the gas lantern was lit again and she saw Rory hold it high to survey the camp. Clare was sitting up in her sleeping bag with her eyes wide and startled and one hand flung out dramatically. 'They've been killed,' she gasped. 'Look at it!'

Over Nick's sleeping bag was a tangle of branches, twigs and leaves. The thick butt of a large dry branch had crashed on Sue's sleeping bag and she saw Rory walk forward slowly, his face strained and shadowed, and the light wavered unsteadily in his hand.

'What's happened?' Sue demanded.

Clare shrieked again and the outflung hand went to her

mouth as she saw Sue appear into the circle of light. 'My God! I thought you were dead!'

'Where's Nick?' Sue asked, appalled.

It was ludicrous, after so great a fright, to see his head burrow up through the greenery and see his hair, tousled in a cockatoo crest, emerge from the leaves. 'Get me out of this thing!' he raved.

Rory and Kent rushed across the sand and strained to move the green bough which had fallen on Nick. It had been brought down by the dried, heavy, desiccated limb.

'Are you hurt, mate?' Kent asked anxiously.

Nick put a hand to his head. 'I've had a belt across the ear, I can tell you that.' Twigs crackled and broke as he forced his way clear and he became alarmed when he looked around.

'You camped under a widow-maker, you two,' Kent pointed out soberly.

'I didn't put the bedding here,' Nick protested. 'Rory did.'

There was a silence and Sue shivered, seeing the heavy limb across where she had lain. Kent came across the creek-bed and put his arms about her.

'That was a close go,' he said gently. 'You can thank your lucky stars that you were out of your sleeping bag.'

'I went to get my watch,' she said stupidly. 'It was Mother's and I'd left it on a tree——'

Rory's voice was angry in protest. 'I set your bedding in place in the open! Who moved it?'

Nobody answered. Sue saw the way Nick stared at Rory and the same ugly thought came to her mind. The bedding had been moved so that the tree was above them, and the dangerous and rotted branch lined up where they would be in a position which could lead to death for one—or both. What proof did they have to the contrary? She had heard movements, and Rory was still dressed and had not been to bed, it seemed.

Who else would wish them dead—or out of the way?

A ringer drove the horses to the yards at daybreak and breakfast sizzled on the campfire. Mrs Colter and her son ate their meal apart and she saddled a horse with the men.

Sue walked towards the tall woman with determination. 'You're helping with the muster too, Mrs Colter?'

'Always have,' she said abruptly and with no inflection in her voice.

Sue felt baffled and said feebly, 'You must ride well.'

'I'm bush bred and reared,' was the reply.

Sue wanted to turn and run, but it was no way to get information. 'I'd like to talk to you about Uncle Dryden,' she said.

'There's no point.' Mrs Colter was a stubborn adversary and it made Sue angry and stiffened her resolution.

She said deliberately, 'I feel there is a point. He'd written to Mother and asked us to come. We were not unwanted or uninvited guests, Mrs Colter.'

The woman's eyes were cold and watchful, dark and unreadable. 'You must have been invited, Miss Howard, if you say so.' The implication hung between them, insulting and subtle.

Sue ignored it. 'My brother and I will be visiting Undara, Mrs Colter.'

It was a mistake to face her with a definite defiance. She merely nodded and there was again that hint of pity in her acceptance of the ultimatum.

'You'll have to discuss it with Rory,' she said, and her smile was thin and mocking. 'He's running Undara now, Miss Howard. Had you forgotten?' She flung the reins over the head of her mount and swung herself into the saddle with a lithe quickness which gave no indication of her age. She looked down at the girl and her voice was curt and unfriendly.

'What's the use of going to Undara now, Miss Howard?'

She rode away, whipcord-tough, thin and strong. Her spirited horse was reined in hard and her hands were firm on the reins. Sue watched her go, and saw the lively mounts subdued one by one by the stockmen before they left the yards.

Clare's mouth drooped as she stifled a yawn. 'These hellish hours! I didn't know there *was* a six a.m.! You'd better ride with me, Sue.'

'I won't be far away,' Sue promised.

She mounted the quiet brown horse led out for her. It was a pleasant ride through the morning hours while the earth was cool and the air clear, but as the heat increased the girls found it tiring. The cattle moved slowly, sunlight touching a horned head or reddening a haunch, and lowing, came to the girls across the space between.

'Not too close,' Clare commanded, 'I'm not riding in their dust.'

When lunch time drew near again the cattle were some distance ahead of Sue and Clare. Rory cantered towards his guests and his face was dusty and his horse sweat-covered.

Clare's smile was wintry. 'We haven't seen much of you.'

He nodded agreement. 'It's important that we get a clean muster. There are a lot of broken gullies in the hills and we have to scour them thoroughly. You'll be looking forward to your lunch. Hello, who's this?'

A small plane appeared over the low eroded hills, dropped lower to skim over the cattle and caused them to grow uneasy. Sue saw the ringers, in charge of the mob, urging their horses to a canter and stragglers being forced back from breaking away.

'Blasted fool!' Rory snapped explosively.

The small, expensive aircraft dropped lower, tilted, zoomed over their heads and dropped to the surface of a claypan ahead. Clare reined her horse in hard and Sue saw the rangy chestnut which Rory rode today rear and thresh the ground with its forefeet before going into a wild fusillade of bucks. Her own concentration was diverted and it took little to unseat her. The quiet mount swerved away as dust blew up from the exhaust of the plane, and Sue realised that she was off balance. She grabbed at the mare's mane and the pommel of the saddle and felt her fingers slip. Then she was down, with an aching crash which jolted the breath from her body.

She gasped and saw the plane dwindle as it taxied away, to turn and begin to return to them.

Rory flung himself from the saddle and dropped the reins to the ground. The horse, so intractable a few minutes before, stood as though tied. The bushman's set and furious face was the first thing Sue saw when she opened her eyes.

She thought despairingly, if he begins to rage at me I shall cry. He must think I'm a nuisance and a bore...

His voice was very close to her ear as he bent to lift her and she felt a weakness which was not the result of the fall, as he held her close. She felt strangely comforted and secure as his arms enfolded her. 'Are you all right?' he asked quickly.

She nodded and drew a few deep breaths. 'I'm not a very good rider,' she admitted, mortified.

He looked away from her towards the short, stocky man who had climbed down from the plane and his voice was harsh in condemnation of the visiting pilot. 'I'll tell that young idiot a thing or two——'

Sue stood erect, suddenly self-conscious, and saw the

grim line of his mouth as he caught her quiet mare and led her close. 'Do you want a boost up?' he asked.

'No, thanks.'

She could not risk his touch again and the strange emotions it aroused in her. He did not argue, but joined Clare, and they stood together as the pilot came closer and spoke breezily. 'I say, that was stupid of me——'

'It was a damned fool thing to do!' Rory snapped.

'You have cause to be annoyed, old man,' he smiled at Sue. 'I hope you're not hurt.' The shrewd hazel eyes in the round face were confident that his apology would be accepted.

'I'm only shaken,' Sue replied stiffly.

He came closer and took her hand. 'I deserve a belt over the ear for that. It didn't occur to me that the horses——'

'It should have,' Rory's voice was level. 'You shouldn't have a licence to fly!'

'Oh, fair go—I'm sorry, Rory! I seem to have started off on a wrong note.'

The older man stared at him. 'Good grief, it's you, Gerry!'

'Dad sent me off to have a look round our places,' Gerry beamed, 'I thought I'd drop in for lunch.'

'You would!'

The irony was lost on Gerry. He was out of place in the Outback, his clothing smart and tailored, city-style. He had a smooth, facile handsomeness owing much to the good tailoring, for he was short and there was a hint of puffiness in the round face.

They walked forward with him, leading their horses, and Clare was sarcastic. 'Do you always drop in like this and frighten everything in sight?' she demanded. He smiled flashily. 'Only when they're ridden by charming girls.'

He scanned Sue's face slowly as though memorising her

71

features. Clare slipped an arm through Rory's and said plaintively, 'I can't ride another yard.'

'Go in with Kent.' He glanced across at the approaching vehicle. 'I asked him to come back for you both.'

When Kent pulled in beside him they were introductions and talk, then the men looked the trim aircraft over, but Sue felt there was a reserve in Rory's manner. He had to accept the young man as the son of an old friend, evidently, but he did not like him.

Snatches of conversation came to her as Gerry Darker explained quickly. 'Flying up to Waneroo ... on to Blue Gum for the Picnic Races ...'

'Don't you ever *work*?' A dry comment from Rory.

'You'd better come in to camp in the Rover.' Kent's voice.

'Then I'll nip over to the Northern Territory before I go back to Sydney,' from Gerry.

'You live in the city?' Clare asked.

'Is there anywhere else to live?' he replied with mocking cheerfulness. He turned to Sue with the swift, easy smile. 'You don't look like a country girl.'

It would be obvious, Sue conceded bitterly. My face sunburned and haggard with weariness, covered in dust...

'She's English,' Clare said scathingly.

Gerry took out a gold cigarette case and offered it round. Nobody smoked except Clare. He flicked a monogrammed lighter for her.

'Taxi over closer to the trees.' Rory was in command again. 'We'll tie your plane down there.'

'Are you coming in with me, Sue?' Kent asked.

'She is.' Rory took the reins from her hand. 'You, too, Clare.'

Clare pretends to enjoy his bossiness, Sue fumed, but I don't have to! She glared at him as he slipped the saddles

off and placed them in the vehicle, followed them with the
bridles, and mounted swiftly in the quick, sliding movement which had him in the saddle before his horse was
aware of it. He nodded curtly to Gerry. 'I'll see you at
lunch.'

The words could have been welcoming, but were not, but
Sue seemed to be the only one who sensed it. Kent waited,
a camera ready, to watch the plane trundle over the baked
earth, but did not press the shutter. He turned away after a
moment.

'He thinks he owns the earth,' Clare commented.

Kent shrugged. 'A good slice of it.'

They followed the plane to the belt of trees and here the
house-party had a quick lunch. As Rory poured the billy tea
and dispensed hospitality with an unconscious air of confidence, Sue studied him unobserved. He had a natural
poise and dignity; he's at ease wherever he is, she admitted
bleakly, disliking him, yet trying to be fair. He's master of
himself . . .

Gerry leaned against the bole of the coolibah after he had
eaten, a mug of tea in one manicured hand, a cigarette in
the other. 'Is your muster progressing well?' he asked.

'Fair enough,' Rory said laconically.

'The old man wants me to get fresh stock for Waneroo.'
It was an unspoken offer.

'Who would inspect them?' Rory asked scathingly.

Gerry laughed lightly as though accepting the veiled in-
sult.

'Not me, as you can guess. I'm no judge. I'll send my
manager over if you're interested——'

The cattle man was brief. 'Thanks, no.'

'Do you come to the Inland often, Mr Darker?' Clare
began.

'Call me Gerry,' he said breezily. 'No, I don't come

73

often.' His gaze returned to Sue again. 'Though I may have cause to return this way——'

Sue took no notice, but Clare said positively, 'Sue and Nick are only here for a few days. They're returning to the city then.'

He said heartily to Sue and Nick, 'You must let me look after you. I could fly you down to Sydney, perhaps? I'll call in on my way back from the north.'

Rory said suddenly, 'Well, we won't keep you, Gerry.' He moved decisively as though to end the meeting.

Nick interposed swiftly, 'That could be very useful, eh, Sue? We'll both be job-hunting when we hit town.'

Gerry put his drink down and fumbled in his hip pocket. 'Here. This is my address in Sydney, phone number and so on—I might be able to help you into something.'

Nick took the card eagerly, his face lighting up at the thought of an exciting future. Sue wished he would not be so transparently young and obvious in his rush to be friendly. Gerry turned to her, hand outstretched in the confident gesture of one who is sure of his place in the world.

'I'll say au revoir, not goodbye, Sue. I'll see you again.'

'Perhaps, perhaps not.' Her head was held proudly.

Her resistance seemed to please him and there was a secret and approving smile behind the hazel eyes.

Rory's face looked stern as he moved away and Gerry followed. They went from the tree shadow to blinding sunlight together.

'He fell for you, Sue,' Kent observed cheerfully.

Clare spoke sharply. 'I think he's a self-satisfied bore!'

'A very wealthy bore,' Kent agreed maliciously.

'It's no sin to have money,' Nick argued with a frown. 'It strikes me that money is worshipped out here in Australia.'

'You know where to go if you don't like it,' Clare said offensively.

74

The motor of the plane began to roar and soon the air-craft taxied away from them and became airborne. It swung back to dip over the trees and began to climb. The chestnut started in fright and the wild eyes showed white as he tossed his head.

'Young fool!' Rory was curt when he came back.

'Does he own several properties?' Nick enquired.

'His father made the money,' Rory said with a hint of contempt, 'he spends it. A man who runs his properties from a penthouse in Sydney isn't interested in the good of his land.'

'It sounds a pretty comfortable way of life,' declared Nick.

Clare pushed damp tendrils of hair away from her fore-head. 'What are we to do this afternoon, Rory?' she wanted to know.

'I'll take you girls on to the night camp, if you like,' Kent offered. 'The light is no good just now. I'll have a sweet and dreamless sleep,' he added, unashamed, 'while you battle with the heat and the flies out there, Rory.'

The bushman's firm white teeth showed in amusement as his bronzed face creased in laughter. 'I envy you, Kent.' There was no trace of it in his voice as he turned to Nick. 'Let's away.'

Nick was tired and the hard riding had been an ordeal for him. He hesitated briefly, tempted to stay with the others and have the rest he craved, but the faintly raised eyebrow stung his pride. 'I'm coming,' he said, furious with himself for wishing to impress a man he hated.

'It hasn't taken Gerry long to get out of sight,' Clare observed.

'It doesn't take Gerry long to get what he wants,' Kent put in. 'He's a shrewd boy!'

'He's no fool,' Rory admitted. 'I don't admire his busi-

75

ness tactics, though. You remember Jack Chapman, Kent? He put him off his property with no scruples whatever, when the mortgage fell due. A sharp dealer, that one!'

And what, Sue felt like saying, were the tactics that won Undara for you?

CHAPTER FOUR

THE site for the night camp was a wide bed of sand ringed by a stony outcrop. It was a kilometre or so from a lonely windmill, tank and troughing. Broken boulders were upthrust from iron-hard ground, but within them was a clearing where the cook had stretched awnings between stunted trees, one for his kitchen activities and another for general shelter. The heat was concentrated and intense.

Clare's face was scarlet and her temper very short as she surveyed it. 'Look at that!' she snapped. 'What a place to spend the afternoon! Surely there's a cool spot somewhere?'

'Not within cooee,' Kent said, unruffled.

He stretched out on his bedroll under the shade of his car and Sue knew that it would be little cooler there. In a short time he was asleep; she envied him as she sprayed fly repellant round her face and tried to rest. If only Clare would not complain so incessantly!

After a time Sue picked up her hat and walked across to the cook where her offer of help was accepted; she found he was more eager for company than the token task he set her. She stayed there until he made a 'cuppa', as he called it. She carried the steaming mugs and plate of buttered brownie over to Clare and to Kent. 'The cattle are coming,' she called cheerfully.

Kent rolled out swiftly and reached for his tea. 'The light will be right soon. That golden glow outlining the beasts—Want to come, Sue?'

'I'd like to, thanks.'

Clare lit another cigarette and yawned. 'I'm not coming.'

'You weren't asked,' Kent replied in the same tone.

It passed the next hour or two, and Sue found Kent's work interesting. When he came back to the car after he had taken the last photograph he leaned in the window of the car and his hand was gentle under her chin.

'You're a good mate, little Sue.' He kissed her. Past his head Sue saw the rangy chestnut come alongside and Rory looked down on them. His voice was clipped.

'Don't let me interrupt you, but it's time to go to the camp. We're holding the cattle on the bore tonight. There are no yards.'

Kent withdrew his head slowly. 'We're on our way.'

Rory cantered away and Sue stared after him. He seemed forbidding. It was no wonder, she admitted sadly, after what Nick had said to him. They wouldn't be able to be friends, ever ... She felt regret, for some reason as though she had missed something precious and of value. It's not a friendly war, she thought. We're outsiders and he'll keep us there.

At the campfire Sue found herself beside the tall, thin man who had been pointed out to her as Sim Colter. She made an opportunity to speak to him and told him quickly who she was. He watched her face intently and the thin lips parted in a brief smile, but before he could reply a hard brown hand touched his arm and his mother stood between them. There was an ironic look in her eyes.

'More beef, Miss Howard?'

'No, thank you,' Sue said, keeping disappointment out of her voice.

She had to go on eating, pretending that it didn't matter, but dismay was growing in her. These people were united in their efforts to get rid of them! She seemed to be isolated, temporarily, as though the others had moved away from her with the Colters. Then she saw that a man deliberately came from the group to join her. The bright light showed that he was stout and florid and his checked shirt strained over his abdomen. His small blue eyes were deep-set, slitted from the harsh light of the region where his life had been spent.

As he came towards her Sue noticed the lightness of his walk, his big frame balanced forward on the toes of his elastic-sided riding boots in a bow-legged walk which spoke of years of riding. He spoke in a soft drawl. 'You must be the English gel.'

'Yes, I'm Sue Howard.' She had to look up to him and into the light so that he seemed blurred and indistinct against the brilliance.

'I'm from Undara. Frank Waters is the name.'

'I'm so pleased to meet you, Mr Waters.'

'Everyone calls me Frank,' he said. 'We don't go for fancy handles to our names out here.'

She smiled at him warmly. 'You knew my uncle well, Mr—er—Frank?'

'Yeah, you could say that,' he said heavily. 'We were mates. You could say I knew him.'

She moved so that she could observe him and saw the lines bitten into the fleshy face where time and dry air had eroded the skin. She gained an impression that his mouth hardened when he spoke, though there was affability in his manner.

'I hope we can talk,' she said eagerly and anxiously. 'My

78

brother and I have come so far to visit our uncle. It's been a shock to find that he's dead.'

Her expectancy was replaced by baffled fury when he said flatly, 'You'd be best to go home again, miss. Yeah, it would be the wisest thing. You didn't know him alive—why bother him now he's dead? You'd best go.'

She looked after him in exasperation. This was what Nick meant by a conspiracy of silence and secrecy! What was the matter with everyone? Why were the newcomers being urged away from Undara?

When they laid out their bedding Nick said in a low voice, 'There'll be no accidents tonight, Sue. I'll see to that.'

The sandy circle inside the big stones was sheltered and appeared cosy in the firelight. The Land Rover and Kent's car were parked outside the broken rocks as space was limited. Sue heard a man singing as he rode round the cattle and a small thrill touched her spine. This was the life she had dreamed of! The lowing of the restless beasts and the clatter of hooves on stones created an uneasy undertone in the distance.

The moon had not risen and bells jingled as horses cropped herbage nearby. Hobbies clinked and a hoof struck stone occasionally. In the herd a cow bellowed monotonously for a weak calf which had been taken by a dingo. The sound was abrasive and saddening.

Sue heard Clare ask, 'What do you do with the cattle, Rory?'

'We'll draft tomorrow. That means cutting out the fat stock by riding a good camp horse into the herd and bringing out the chosen beasts. These will be held in a separate mob to go into the yards at the homestead. The others will be dispersed to other paddocks where the feed is good.'

'What do you do with the fat ones?'

79

Without turning Sue could picture her, leaning against his knee, her expression one of absorbed interest.

'Sell them. The road trains, large diesel trucks, will load them from the yards and take them to market in the south. That's where the money comes from!'

Her light laugh sounded pleased. 'That's the part I like!'

For some reason it hurt to hear her possessive accents and know that she was the one on whom Rory smiled.

In the distance storm clouds hung low and there was a rumble of thunder intermittently. Rory remarked that it was a 'dry storm', and the talk turned to other things.

Sue was almost asleep, lulled by the singing, the sounds of the night, and her weariness, when she felt a touch on her shoulder.

'Sue. Sue!' whispered Nick urgently. She snapped to wakefulness and he leaned closer to her ear. 'Get up. We're going to move.'

She eased herself out of the bag, shivering in the chill outside and he half lifted, half slid her bundle of bedding. Now and again he stopped to listen lest the slither of canvas on sand should rouse the sleepers about the dying fire.

When they were behind the Land Rover he whispered, 'I'm not sleeping close to that lot, Sue. Somebody there is trying to do us in, and I'm not saying that Mr Rory Stevens is innocent!'

She felt dazed with weariness and wished he need not indulge his passion for drama at such odd hours. 'Oh, Nick, not now! It's far too late and I'm tired——'

'We'll move our bedding, Sue. I'm going to camp out here in the open. Keep close.' He moved into the dark with her bedroll bundled into his arms in an awkward heap.

'You left my torch—my things are back there.'

'Keep your voice down,' he said sharply and importantly. 'They won't know we're out here.'

Afterwards Sue tried in vain to get the humps and bumps out of her bed, but Nick had flung her groundsheet over stones on the ground. Her ire began to rise. She managed to dislodge several of the lumps and settle herself again, but as the stars blurred before her weary eyes, her discomfort and her annoyance grew stronger. Once Nick got some bee in his bonnet he was unbearable! They had to lie on stones because he thought they'd be safer out there! Anyone could have seen them go from the circle at the fire. The men weren't so far away—anyone watching——

The moon had risen but was obscured by low clouds and it seemed very dark without its glow. Sue sat up, half-inclined to wake Nick and tell him that she was going back to a more comfortable situation, but was prevented by the niggle of unease which had been with her all day. The branch lying across her bedding had been an ugly and frightening sight. Could one be hated—or feared—enough for such a death? Had it been an accident?

She lay back and tried again to go to sleep, but her brain was too alert and she could not rest. She did not know how much time had passed when the ground reverberated under her body and she heard a shout. The quiet of the night was broken by a noise which increased and became like thunder. She could not imagine what it could be. It seemed to be part of the earth, part of the night.

Hooves? The click of hooves on stones made her alert, but the darkness hid the danger from her. She was too inexperienced to realise what was happening. She heard Rory shout from the camp and a man's voice answer, and she fought to free the zipper of her sleeping bag. This time she was the one to wake Nick, and she shook him urgently while the sound built up and came closer and closer.

'Nick, the cattle! The cattle!'

It seemed an interminable period of time before he rallied, and then he turned his head aside and refused to be disturbed. She had to scream at him, fear making her voice high above the increasing rumble. He, too, had to fight his way free, impeded by sleep and clumsiness, and Sue had a sudden terrible impression of tossing horns against the stars and the rattle of rushing cloven hooves.

The cattle were upon them.

Sister and brother lurched towards the Land Rover, a bulk and a haven, and tried to crawl under it. Sue felt the vehicle rock as a great, crashing body fell against it, and there was a wild bellow as a beast went down. Dust eddied about them and sparks flashed from stones as the mob passed. Stragglers pounded behind to catch up and the dust cloud deepened to suffocating proportions.

'I'm hurt,' Nick gasped, his voice shaking, 'my arm, Sue. I can't move it.'

She lay on the ground, a pain spearing into her head, and nausea and faintness rolled over her until blackness enveloped her completely.

When she regained consciousness she saw Clare standing at a window, and the dark-haired girl turned languidly. 'I thought you must be coming round. You've been muttering a bit. How's the head?'

Sue stared at her. 'Muzzy.' She tried not to ask the hackneyed question, 'Where am I?' but dazed as she was, her surroundings seemed strange and unfamiliar.

'You gave us a fright, the pair of you, out there with the cattle. We can't figure out what possessed you—but for the Land Rover they'd have trampled you, the rocks protected the camp, though.'

The cattle ... It revived memory and Sue felt pain stab behind her eyes as she opened them wide. 'Nick?' she gasped.

'Oh, we've had a drama here,' Clare said with relish. 'A

rush to the homestead to the radio-transceiver, and the Flying Doctor landing on the strip by the lights of any vehicles we could muster. It certainly livened things up!'

Sue tightened her lips, knowing that Clare's part in the activities would be fully recounted before any mention was made of Nick.

'That doctor is a charmer,' Clare went on. 'I wished I'd been the one to go to hospital!'

'Is Nick——?'

'He said I did a very good job,' Clare said, pleased.

'Nick did?'

'No, the doctor said it. It's the sort of thing I'll have to do when I'm married, of course.'

'Will you tell me about Nick!' Sue snapped, exasperated.

'Heavens, don't get in a paddy! I'm just telling you about driving the car and lining the lights up so——' Seeing Sue's expression Clare said stiffly, 'Oh, Nick's all right. Why wouldn't he be?'

'He's in hospital?'

'Whisked off to have X-rays and whatever. You had a bang on the head but no complications, so Rory ordered Mrs Settler to bed you down here.'

'There was no need for that,' Sue protested. 'I should have gone with Nick.'

Clare shrugged. 'You're here, and that's that.' Evidently she had not been in agreement with the idea.

She wore a dark blue dress bound with white on neck and sleeves and her hair was shining and freshly set. She was more at home in the gracious homestead than she had been in the harsh outdoors. She yawned again openly and Sue said apologetically, 'I must have been a nuisance. I'll soon be fit again.'

She must join Nick, wherever he was. There was no

choice. It seemed they were not to go to Undara, and she accepted it, too tired to care. Nick was lying in hospital in a strange town, alone. She must go to him.

Clare did not linger and Sue did not try to detain her. She lay and watched the blue sky beyond the window and felt a fit of nervous depression seize her. She felt alone and vulnerable with Nick so far away, yet knew that if he were here he would be no comfort to her.

The light dimmed gradually and she heard firm and decisive footsteps on the concrete floor of the wide verandah. Knuckles rapped at the surround of the screened door to the bedroom. She murmured assent and watched the tall man as he came to stand where Clare had stood at the foot of the bed.

Sue's heart pounded. A sick dread filled her when he arrived, but whether it was fear of him or fear of his attraction for her, she did not know. She lay still and looked at him as he stood with a powerful brown forearm laid along the high wooden bed-end.

There was a magnetism that flashed between them, she had to admit bleakly, physical, powerful and dangerous. This man is my enemy, she reminded herself. I must be wary of him.

'Are you feeling better?' he asked curtly.

'Thank you, yes.'

'The Flying Doctor checked your injuries. You should be right in a day or two.'

'I appreciate your kindness,' she answered stiffly. He had said to Kent, 'They'll be nothing but a handicap to you . . .'

'The hospital was pushed for beds,' he explained. 'There's a 'flu epidemic in town.'

'So you had no choice,' she said. Why, oh, why did she have to try to sting him?

'I had a choice.' His voice was level. 'I chose that you

84

should stay here. Clare was available to care for you.'

'Clare?'

Her eyes widened, remembering hands sponging her body, moving her gently. It did not seem Clare's field.

'And Mrs Settler,' he added.

'Mrs Settler, of course.' Her voice grew stronger. 'I like Marj.'

He was dry. 'She likes you, it seems. She said you were no trouble.'

Sue's eyes were cornflower blue in her pale face. 'I'm sorry to have caused an upset to the household.'

He ignored her apology. 'I've been in touch with the Flying Doctor and Nick's arm is set and in plaster. He'll be out of hospital as soon as it's comfortable.'

'I'll go and join him.' Her disheartened attitude coloured her words. 'They're right, all of them. We should have stayed at home.'

He spoke cuttingly, 'It's late in the day to think of that. You're here and have stirred up a hornet's nest with your reckless probing and prying.'

She tried to infuse sarcasm into her voice. 'If you would tell me what I want to know there would be no need, would there?'

'Have you forgotten that I'm the accused, Sue?' A muscle worked beside his mouth for a moment and his smile was mirthless.

She felt too tired to fight him and her words were low. 'Perhaps we could start again?'

'I shall be happy to go into the question of Undara with you when you're well,' he said coldly.

She watched him as he spoke, and she was trying to identify his character. The stiff politeness of his face defeated her. He walked away and did not look back as he went.

Sue threw the light cover aside and swung her legs over the side of the bed and tried to stand. The room swung and dipped, but after a moment she felt more normal and walked experimentally to the door.

Marj Settler, tray in hand, found her there and her good-natured face was concerned. 'Heavens, don't overdo it, Miss Howard!'

Sue laughed breathlessly. 'I'm determined to walk to the bathroom myself, Marj. I want to get strong again.'

'I'll wait around and give you a hand,' Marj offered. 'I brought your dinner.' She placed the tray on the table and followed with an anxious expression that made Sue laugh. However, she was glad of a supporting arm back to bed when she had had her wash.

'This won't do,' she said, mortified. 'I'll have to get going.'

'Don't you hurry on my account,' Marj said warmly.

'You're so busy, Marj. This big place to care for, the cooking and your twins—I haven't met them. May I?'

Marj looked pleased. 'They'd love to come and say hello, Miss Howard. They're having their tea now. I have a girl to help me in busy times—the Boss gets one of the aboriginal girls to come over from Manchie Downs. She's mission-trained and very good.'

Sue had lifted the covers of the silver dishes and surveyed the succulent brown roast, sliced thinly, flanked by the crisply browned potatoes and fresh greens. 'Doesn't it look tempting!' she cried appreciatively.

'The Boss cut your meat so I could bring it in before the others start.'

Sue felt her throat tighten unbearably. She could picture the big man sharpening the knife, as he had done on the first night, slicing the roast expertly and with precision. He had cut it for her...

86

As he would for any guest under his roof, she reminded herself, and picked up her knife and fork. It felt very lonely in the bedroom and she heard the big bell boom out the summons for dinner and the sound of footsteps on the verandah. Then silence. The thick walls were a barrier to sound. She could hear no tinkle of glass or clink of silver, no voices.

She ate the meat course. The sweet, too, was attractive in the stemmed bowl of fine crystal, but she ate the iced fruit and cream with scant appetite. What an idiot she was! Lapped in comfort with delectable food, beautifully served, and feeling near to tears. She put the tray aside and took up her coffee cup. After she had drunk it she lay back, waiting for the night to come, and willing herself to be well.

Why do Rory and I grate on each other? she wondered. His attitude to us in the beginning raised a barrier before we began; then Nick's suspicions loudly and foolishly voiced, were a disaster. What might he have said when he was in pain with his arm, convinced that there had been foul play?

They were separated now, she and Nick, whether by accident or design. She was alone and they had not reached or viewed, their destination, Undara. Her previous decision to give up had been put aside; it had been born of weakness and shock. She must go there, she must! The answer to it all was there ... Nick or no Nick, she'd go there somehow!

Perhaps Kent would take her now, or Rory. Surely that was reasonable enough? A small thing to ask as a matter of sentiment—to see her uncle's home.

To refuse to go on would be cowardly. She owed it to her uncle, and to Nick, to face whatever was hidden at Undara. She must keep fear from swamping her and her resolution strong, and she must sleep. She had to be fit again before the next move could be made.

Kent arrived in jauntily, coffee cup in hand. He had bathed and changed for dinner and his narrow face had become deeply tanned. He sat on the bed beside her and took her hand. 'Well, little Sue, you look brighter.'

'I'll be up tomorrow,' she told him.

'Don't be too sure. Rory will tell you what to do.'

He will not! Sue thought decidedly, but hid her thoughts. 'What have you done today?' she asked.

He looked downcast. 'Blasted camera played up. The film was stuck, it had cracked with the heat and got wound round the reels. Talk about a mess! All that lot will be lost.'

'Oh, Kent, what a shame!' She was looking at him with sympathetic concern when Rory came to the door quiet in his lighter shoes. He stood and watched them for a moment without speaking, then said, 'I'll say goodnight, Sue. If there's anything you want, ask Clare.'

Ask Clare, indeed! As if that spoiled young lady would be doing anything to help!

When Rory had gone Kent spoke again. 'He was livid about the cattle, Sue. They're quiet and well-handled. We can't make out what caused the rush.'

She did not want to remember it. 'Let's forget it.'

He frowned at her, the unruly lock of hair falling forward as he bent towards her. 'What on earth were you doing out there?' he demanded.

'It seemed so stony where we'd been lying,' she said lamely, 'Nick thought it might be better there.'

It was the silliest of stories, the weakest of excuses, but Kent accepted it as due to their ignorance of the country.

His laugh was indulgent. 'It would be just as bad out

88

there, Sue. You can't get away from stones in that area.'

She said swiftly, 'Did the cut-out take place?'

'The drafting? Yes. The fats were cut out and will be walked to the homestead yards tomorrow.'

'Where are the yards? I haven't seen them.'

'A distance away over the hills. Rory keeps the dust away from the house.'

'I might be well enough to see the cattle loaded in the trucks,' Sue said hopefully.

'You might. Ask Rory.'

She said forcibly, 'I will not ask Rory!' She snatched her hand away from his grasp. 'What has he to do with my decisions?'

Kent stood up. 'Heck! Trust me to wear you out!' As if she were putting on a tired tantrum! He added remorsefully, 'I only meant that he's responsible for you. The doctor left you in his charge, that's all. It isn't fair to him for you to go running round in the heat and undoing the care you've had.'

Sue felt mean. 'I am snappy, aren't I? Sorry, Kent.'

He leaned down and kissed her lightly. 'Um-um! You smell lovely. Like a flower.'

She tried to laugh. 'Poetic!'

He grinned at her from the door. 'I have quite a vein of poetry in me. You wait and see, Sue, my love.'

When Sue had showered and dressed the next morning the big house was quiet. The men had gone out to the paddock and Marj told her, in a expressionless voice, that Clare was asleep.

The grey-eyed twins, John and James, regarded Sue from under thatches of whitish blond hair. They were round-faced, freckled and solemn in their first shyness with her. She sat at the kitchen table and talked to them, and

Marj, moving from stove to sink, said after a while, 'It's easy to see you like kids, Miss Howard.'

'Yes,' agreed Sue, 'I should have taken up teaching instead of secretarial work.'

'The Boss gets fed up with office work, I know,' Marj said with an affectionate laugh.

Sue shyed away from speaking of Rory. 'What do the children do while you're busy, Marj?' she queried.

'Old Mrs Travers cares for them. Dan is the men's cook—you met him? She's not able to get about easily owing to her arthritis, but she minds them for me. Their cottage is the last one behind the big shed.'

'I haven't seen over the homestead area,' said Sue.

'No. The Boss has been busy, but he'll show you round when he gets time.' Marj seemed to think that Sue was an honoured guest and this, again, was a topic which must be avoided. When the small boys ran off across the brown earth to the line of trees which shielded the cottages, Marj watched them go and her mouth drooped.

'I wish I had more time to be with them,' she sighed.

'Yes, you must,' Sue agreed.

Marj began to wash her cooking utensils. 'I'm lucky I've had my job and could keep them with me.'

'You have no family, Marj?'

'No, I'm an orphan. I was desperate when Cec died, I can tell you.'

Sue took up a towel.

'Leave that,' the young woman urged. 'Go and rest.'

Sue smiled. 'I'll rest later. I must get strong!'

She needed to be strong and regain her health. Tomorrow...

Clare lay in bed most of the day, and Sue ate her lunch at the big table alone. The room seemed to echo the clink of her knife and fork and she kept her eyes on the sunlit garden beyond the verandah and tried not to think of the events of the past week.

Marj had come and fetched her and stood by while she sent a message over the radio transceiver to Nick in hospital. It seemed a frail link, and no real comfort without his voice in answer to her own. There was no plane going through in that direction until the end of the week so that she could not fly out, even if she wished. She did not intend to. Schooling herself to a desperate patience, she lay and rested during the afternoon, and did not rise until Marj brought the afternoon tea to the front verandah.

Clare had showered and wore smart lounging pyjamas which bore the stamp of Paris; obviously her many suitcases had arrived on some passing transport. She was exotic in the vivid colours and one bare shoulder was seductive and rounded above the daringly cut bodice. It was a revealing and unsuitable outfit for the surroundings.

She poured tea for them both and inspected the cake and biscuits critically. 'That cook will have to pull herself up a bit when I'm running things,' she commented.

Sue stared at her. 'Marj? She's an excellent cook, Clare.'

'A plain cook. I like elaborately prepared food. You wouldn't understand. You've lived a very narrow life, I gather, but Daddy moves in good circles overseas and I'm accustomed to style in the service I receive. I demand it.'

'I'm sure she does her best,' Sue defended. 'The biscuits are crisp and tasty and the cake looks feather-light.'

'She'll have to go,' decided Clare. 'I'll get Rory to get a trained chef for the homestead.'

Sue straightened. 'Marj has twins to keep. She needs the job.'

'More fool her! She should have used her head and not had children.'

'Rory won't sack her, I'm sure.' Sue spoke from a feeling of conviction.

Angry colour tinged Clare's cheekbones and her cup clattered to the saucer. Her voice was ominous. 'Are you telling *me* what Rory will or won't do?'

Sue did not know what mad impulse had led her to say what she had; she had no right to argue with Clare about how the house was to be run or how Rory would react to changes. She got to her feet quickly. 'I'll go for a walk.'

She hurried to her room and got her big hat. She felt that she would quarrel with Clare if she stayed near her.

How does Rory handle her? His usual bulldozing tactics, I suppose, Sue thought sarcastically as she walked along the concrete paths to the side gate. She isn't honest with him, though. The sweet, biddable personality she presents is not the real Clare. What fights they'll have when she shows her true personality!

It wasn't her business. Why should the thought of it fill her with bitter dissatisfaction?

She was about to check the lie of the land and try to form a plan to get to Undara. The track led past the store, which opened at certain hours for the hands to buy extras or needed supplies. Past the quarters at the back of the house where the windows of the men's dining room overlooking her path. At the big shed she glanced in at the machinery. There were empty spaces for many of the vehicles were out on the run. Beyond the shed was a grove of trees and she saw the cottages, neat, white-painted, gauzed against insects and surrounded by steel-railed netting fences. In one garden she caught a glimpse of the pale hair of Marj's twins.

She felt shy at the thought of walking past the houses and cut across to the other outbuildings and to a gully which dropped behind them. Here a large windmill pumped water to a huge galvanised iron tank set high to reticulate to the gardens. There was a trough for animals to drink from, and hundreds of zebra finches congregated at the water; they sat on the branches of spiny Parkinsonia trees nearby and the dozens of small bodies, apricot-beaked, were like large beads along the branches. The air was alive with their quaint call, 'Parp! Parp! Parp!' as they fluttered, drank and perched.

Sue stood quietly and watched them, but her presence gave no alarm. There was a high netting fence beside the tank, and steel pipes carried water to the enclosed area. There were vegetables in rows, silver beet, beetroot, carrots and other root vegetables which she could recognise. Under roofs of cane grass, laid like thatch between two layers of wire netting, were softer plants, lettuce and salad vegetables. Under another shelter she saw the green-patterned curves of melons among silvery leaves.

The fence was very strong, the gate secured by a stout catch. Comparing the lush growth with the dry country about it, Sue conceded that the security would be needed; the cattle would find the green very tempting.

There was no sign of any gardener, but she realised that this must be one man's duty. This, and the garden at the house, and other odd jobs. There was so much she did not know about the running of Yurla, and would have no chance to find out.

A long hill rose from the dry creek and she walked towards the crest. It was dusty, but there was a coating of tough growth and tiny wildflowers.

Thread-like stalks held brave dots of colour above the inhospitable soil and small insects skipped and jumped away from her feet. She wondered at the marvel of their survival and the tenacity of their life cycle in the hard surroundings.

From the crest she could see the house and outbuildings clearly, and the greenery which made the surroundings pleasant. She could see, too, that there was a large water-hole beyond the garden on the northern side where Rory's office and bedroom were situated. She saw the metallic sheen of a large sheet of water set about by gum trees and coolibahs. It must be a considerable expanse, for much of it was hidden by the fall of the banks.

I must walk there later, she thought. She turned to the east and saw a river of cattle flow from the folded hills. They poured from a narrow opening and spread into a fan formation on the plain, and behind and beside them rode the stockmen.

Sue felt a thrill of pleasure. She stood, tense and upright, as she strained to see into the distance. The cattle were coming! These were the cattle coming to the homestead yards to be trucked away. Kent had mentioned yards, but she could see none. They must be over a fold of ridge, somewhere beyond her vision.

The men would be home before long. As she turned to go she saw how the tracks radiated away from the side gate of the homestead and from the big shed, a cobweb of tracks. These drew together as they left the proximity of the buildings, and then speared out into the open country in various directions.

They were pressed into the earth, clear against the rough, stubbled grass and low spiky growth, threads of sun-coloured lines radiating to all points of the compass. Which was the track to Undara?

She studied them attentively, trying to memorise the map-like layout below. It could be important to know which road to take. The west lay to her left, the red ball of sinking sun made that an easy deduction, so the south lay behind her. She turned and faced in that direction again and could hear, on the evening breeze, the cattle lowing as they quickened their steps towards water.

She turned and began to hurry away, confused by the thought that Rory might have seen her figure there, outlined against the sky, and suspect that she was spying on him.

She was hot and flushed by the time she closed the garden gate and was glad Clare was not on the verandah to observe her. She had a shower and dressed slowly, feeling lethargic and disheartened.

She wore a simple dress, a straight, light-weight woollen frock of good cut and design. Her eyes were enhanced by the sky-blue of the material. She did not see the men until they, too, had showered and changed. Kent was buoyant and exuberant, and flung his arms about her as he came out to the verandah.

'How are you now, sweetie? Rested?'

She extricated herself from his embrace, hearing footsteps behind her as Rory carried out a tray of bottles and glasses. He did not smile at her, but his glance was sharp and assessing. She felt the irrational impulse to prod him into some reaction, other than polite indifference. 'As you see, I'm fully recovered.'

'Not fully,' he said curtly. 'Drinks, everyone? Clare——?'

There was a small hush for a moment when she made her entrance. It was an entrance, deliberately late, so that they were gathered there before she came. Kent whistled, but it was more in mockery than approval. Rory glanced across and did not pause in uncorking the bottle in his hand. He made no comment and Sue, who had felt earlier that the outfit was out of place, felt a little sorry for Clare. Both men had reacted badly and it must have disappointed her.

The conversation became general and when the bell rang

for dinner they moved into the big comfortable room and the meal Marj had prepared for them. It was a strange thing, Sue thought, that life seemed to flow back into the house when Rory entered it. All day it had been quiet and now there was laughter, good talk and the excellent meal. She could have enjoyed it so much, had things been different. After dinner they took their coffee to the drawing room where Rory put a match to the stacked logs in the fireplace. The chill of winter crept in when the sun went down.

Kent picked up a glossy magazine from a side table.

'You've not seen my work, Sue,' he said with sudden shyness. He brought the magazine to her and dropped it in her lap in pretended indifference.

'Do they pay well?' Clare asked, with a jibe in her voice. 'Or is it a vanity market?'

'They pay,' Kent said shortly.

His work was the one thing which he did not treat lightly, and Sue sensed his strained attention as she opened the pages. It gave her a thrill to see his name beneath the pictures.

He said quickly, 'I could do better now. I have better cameras, for one thing, and have gained experience——'

Clare drifted across and leaned over the back of the couch so that her hair brushed his cheek. 'They're not bad,' she said condescendingly, 'but you won't be a millionaire on the strength of a few pictures in a magazine, Kent.'

'I have no desire to be a millionaire,' he said curtly.

'They're damned good stuff,' Rory said from the fireplace. 'You captured the feeling of action in the one of the horse-breaker, with the horse just lifting into a buck.'

'They're super!' Sue cried. 'They're wonderful, Kent.'

He looked pleased but said again, 'I could do better now.'

She said warmly, 'One does better with practice, of

course, but there's no need to apologise for these. This one of the little grey donkey—what sad eyes! It's unforgettable!' She studied the group for a moment, the wheeling galah against a twisted branch of hakea, a camel lurching against the loneliness of an empty skyline, and added gently, 'I didn't realise your work was so good, Kent.'

'Where does all that get you, though?' Clare asked again. 'Have you no ambition at all?'

'Not the sort you'd understand!' He glared at her. Rory, crisply, took charge of a situation which was degenerating into a squabble.

'Let's hope you get some pictures as good this time, Kent.' He turned to the fire and said over his shoulder, 'You've given the stockmen a few heart turns over your efforts!'

Kent's laugh was unabashed. 'It's worth the risk if it comes off.'

'I thought you were coming off a few times yourself,' Rory said with a laugh. 'More coffee, Clare?'

He had the situation under control with tact and assurance, and Sue wondered if he would be able to control Clare's temper by such means in the years to come. She was glad when the evening was over and their goodnights were said. As she walked along the verandah she saw the glint of water beyond the garden; the waterhole. There was no cloud to obscure the moon tonight and she could see clearly as she walked towards the fence. Shadows were deep under the native shrubs and she saw the big gum trees silhouetted in black against the bright mirror of the water. She leaned her arms on the metal pipe along the top of the fence and gazed at the scene below.

She heard a quick step behind her and spoke quietly, without turning. 'It's lovely, Kent. This is the type of thing I expected to see in Australia.'

'Would you like to walk down there?'

It was Rory. Not for a moment had she imagined that he would have left Clare and come out to the garden. She stiffened and turned her head.

'I thought it was Kent.'

He ignored the words and gestured to a gate nearby. 'There's a well-worn track. Come along.'

He put out a hand and took hers lightly. She was conscious of his nearness, and tried to close her mind to the magnetism which attracted her.

The track was rough and shadows made ruts appear deeper and holes deceptive and the country was strange and eerie in the frosting of white light. There were large clumps of green, tangled reeds which he told her was lignum and the banks dropped steeply in parts. In others shelved gently to a bed of sand where water caressed the margin. Here they stood together and she slid her hand away. She was conscious of him beside her, breathing evenly, waiting for her to speak.

She said inanely, 'Isn't it quiet?'

'Not at sunset.' There was amusement in his voice. 'That's when the white corellas, the cockatoos, come to rest in the trees. They shriek and change their minds about perches and there's a great to-do until they settle.'

'Are there many birds?'

He pictured the scene for her in his deep, quiet voice. He told her of the life which continually called and flitted over the water in the peace of noon, of the iridescent wings of dragonflies and the green fire of kingfishers. The galahs, in grey and pink, drinking at evening and jostling for positions on the sandy verge. Eagles soaring overhead, and the sombre black crows. Under the enormous stars and in the silence of the night Sue listened, enthralled.

'I should like to see it for myself,' she said simply.

He was silent for a moment and she felt his slight movement away from her. His voice changed. 'You came to see more than this.'

'Undara? Uncle Dryden?'

She regretted having to use the words. The barrier they created was tangible. They were sparring again, hostile and cold.

CHAPTER FIVE

'I MIGHT tell you that your brother has made your views very clear,' Rory said.

Oh, Nick! What *had* he said? As though his first outburst had not been indiscreet enough! Sue tried to keep the discussion calm. 'I'm sorry that he lost his head. He's very impetuous.'

'He's very spoiled and partly it's your fault.'

The attack was so unexpected that she gaped. 'My fault?'

'I guess there's been a loving mother behind the scenes, but the way you carry on the good work is disgusting. Let the boy grow up.'

Hot blood poured into her cheeks. 'I don't spoil him!'

'You wait on him as though he were helpless. You make him selfish.'

'He's accustomed—Mother——' Her voice faltered.

How could she explain that she had had to be the strong one, that her mother, loved as she had been, was sweet, gentle and helpless? As soon as she was old enough, after her father died, Sue had taken over the money side of things or their debts would have crushed them long ago.

Nick had inherited his mother's careless attitude to responsibility, Sue had thought, and she had accepted this as part of his character. To be the strong one was a loneliness of which she was tired.

Yet she was hurt by the accusation that she wanted to keep Nick dependent on her decisions, and her temper flared. 'What do you know of our lives?' she cried.

'I can see for myself that the boy needs responsibility and a firm hand to control him,' Rory retorted.

She was icy. 'Undara might have provided opportunities for him. I had hoped he would find a man's life here in Australia, but that seems impossible under the circumstances.'

'You both arrive at Yurla accusing me——' he began hotly.

'Nick says too much,' she interrupted.

'I agree. The thought must have been there to be expressed, however!'

'If you'd explained at the beginning there might have been no need——' Her voice rose.

'Dryden is dead,' he reiterated. 'There's nothing at Undara that would interest people like you. I'll get my solicitor to give you an accounting of the money side of things——'

'The *money*! I don't want to know about the money! What's the story, that's what I want to know! What's the story behind it all?'

He spoke with terrible bitterness and his eyes gleamed in the moonlight. 'You want to know if I'm responsible for Dryden's death?'

There was a chill deep within her. 'Yes. Yes, that's it, I suppose,' she said hoarsely, and knew, suddenly, that she did not want to know. While there was a doubt she could cling to it, and she knew with dread and certainty that there was to be no evading of the bitter truth.

She had not worn a warm coat and realised that her flesh was cold; she was cold inside and out. She felt the urge to cry out, to tell him not to speak but realised there could be no going back now or the question would hang for ever between them.

Rory was a stranger, hard-faced and strained. His voice was ragged. 'And if I was responsible? What then?'

Her hand crushed the leaves of a shrub and the aromatic smell of tea-tree was on her fingers.

'Are you there, Rory?' Clare called. She had flung a warm, fleecy coat about her shoulders and stood at the top of the bank. Her face grew set as she watched them come towards her. 'What on earth have you been doing?' she demanded.

'Just looking at the water,' Sue muttered.

'You'd better come and have a walk too, Clare,' Rory said tonelessly.

'I thought you'd have asked me in the first place,' she flashed.

Sue muttered a hasty 'goodnight' and left them.

Marj brought breakfast to her in bed and, though Sue felt it had been unnecessary, it gave her a chance to avoid meeting the others. Later she dressed carefully, tough jeans and a light blouse, topped by a heavy jersey which she could doff when the temperature rose. She carried her tray to the kitchen and phrased a question casually. 'What are they doing today, Marj?'

'They're loading the fats for market, Miss Howard. The road trains have arrived and are at the yards now. Are you going out to see the loading?'

'That's a good idea,' Sue said vaguely.

'I'll do up some sandwiches for you and a thermos of tea and you could come back later and have a rest. The Boss and the others have gone ages ago.'

'Where are the yards, Marj?'

'Just follow the track east. You'll see the dust!'

They laughed and Sue went to her room. She gathered up her shady hat and sunglasses and walked across to the big shed. She found Kent there with his head under the uplifted bonnet of the big car; he had taken off the roof rack to repair a weakness in it as well, and it stood against a post nearby.

'Trouble?' she asked anxiously.

'Not now. Just a final check.'

'I thought you'd be out with the others.'

'Rory went out at daybreak and I'm going out with Sim Colter shortly,' he told her.

'In this?' She had to keep her voice casual in case he guessed her intention.

'No, we're going in the Land Rover. Are you coming with us, Sue?'

She pretended to consider. 'Not now. Later, perhaps.'

Kent nodded, wiping a greasy hand absently across his chin and leaving a black smear.

'You're wise. You'd be best to have a quiet day.'

In the shadows at the back of the shed Sue saw the thin, spare man who had been on the muster, brown, sparse and hatchet-faced. 'What do you think of Sim Colter, Kent?' she asked.

'He's a good sheep man and Rory is pleased with his work.'

'And the mother?' she persisted.

'A formidable woman.' Kent had his head bent while he screwed some part of the motor in place. 'Wears the pants in more senses than one, I'd say.'

'What about him? Doesn't he resent it?'

'Quiet Sim? There's no danger of him having an argument with her.' He slapped the bonnet down and patted the mudguard affectionately. 'All set to go.'

'Would you take me to Undara, Kent?' Sue asked.

He nodded. 'We'll go down the track in a few days, Sue. Rory's taking us, and I want to develop some of my film before then. There's a small room I can use here, and Rory said it will be a simple matter to black it out and make a darkroom of it. I want to see what results I'm getting.'

'I hope they turn out well,' Sue said warmly. 'It must be a frightful disappointment when something has gone wrong.'

He grinned. 'You'll see me tearing my hair then! Everything is against photography out here. Heat and dust are hell on film, and insects in the lens! The rough roads are hard on the cameras, too.'

While she listened to him another part of her brain registered the fact that Rory was to take them to Undara. A conducted tour. She watched Kent as he opened the boot and placed the jerry cans of petrol inside. There was a rack on the end wall of the shed where similar cans were stored. He shook each can as he lifted it and the slosh and weight of liquid was reassuring.

'How did you fill them here, Kent?'

'Rory has a bulk supply here. There's a hand bowser at the back of the shed where the vehicles are refuelled, and the tanker comes out from town now and then and fills the underground tank for the station.'

'Everything in a big way,' she said dryly.

He did not note the hint of sarcasm and agreed warmly. 'Yes, Rory's a good bloke and a good manager——'

She came to the back of the car as he lifted the heavy container of water, making her voice light. 'You carry the water and fuel at all times, Kent?'

He agreed absently and closed the boot without locking it. Nobody bothers with locks out here, Sue thought. That's lucky.

'I'm off now, Sue, I want to get pictures of the cattle

103

being loaded. It will be a few days before Nick gets back anyway, and we'll make our plans to go down the track then.'

'Is it so far to Undara?' she asked carefully.

'Westward to the border first—it's only a netting fence. No guard-house there! Then follow the road and, as the bushmen say, "You can't miss it!"' He laughed and squatted down to draw a map in the sand in Outback style, fired by her interest. 'Here's Yurla—this is the track out. Once you're on the road to Undara there's a bore about forty kilometres down the way, another fifty and another bore and a gate. Then you head across the plains due south, a couple of gates, sandhills and a bore——'

Sue strained to follow his sketch and not lose any of the points he made.

'Then you're on Undara.' Kent looked at her cheerfully. 'We'll make it a date, Sue, the next trip, eh?'

She nodded. 'That sounds good, Kent.'

He stretched and yawned. 'Lord! I'm getting tired with these early hours and big days.' He put an arm about her. 'You should forget Undara.'

She was wary. 'Why do you say that?'

'Don't mistake me, Sue, I'm on your side.' His dark eyes were solemn for a moment. 'On your side, little fair girl, but some things are best left undisturbed. Let me take you to Sydney, you can find a niche there, you and Nick——'

Colour flushed her pale face. She was wounded by his words. 'I didn't expect you to turn me down, Kent.' She shook his arm away and stood apart from him. 'Why can't you be honest with me, any of you?'

Kent sobered. 'I'm being honest with you, Sue. I'll take you both to Undara if you want to go, but it's just another homestead, that's all. There's nothing *there*. Can't you see that?'

How could she explain that by seeing the place she might be able to understand the unhappy situation and find out what had caused it? Her mouth twisted. 'It was my uncle's home, Kent. Nick could have been, or should be, his heir, perhaps. I don't *care* about money, but the land—— Did Rory influence my uncle to leave the place to him, or is he just using it for his own ends?'

'Don't ask him questions like that one, Sue!' advised Kent. 'Are you trying to say that he cheated your uncle? He's got a temper, has Rory! Don't accuse him of "undue influence"!'

'You're all loyal to Rory. We're the outsiders,' she observed sadly.

Tears began to well into her eyes, tears of shock, weariness and frustration. He took her agitated hands in his, both of them, and his voice was soothing. 'You're not well yet, Sue darling. You shouldn't be standing about out here. Let me take you back to the house.'

Beneath her feet the markings in the sand became blurred as her eyes watered. A bore ... forty kilometres ... sandhills ... a bore ... It seemed simple enough. She would wait until he had gone with Sim and set out for Undara herself.

Kent escorted her to the house and, as he passed his bedroom, he opened the screen door and flung the car keys towards the dressing table. As they fell, jangling, to the wooden surface Sue kept her face controlled. What colossal luck! She had not thought ahead to how she would get the keys but knew that Kent left them lying around or left them in the car when he was in the bush, a carelessness of which Rory had spoken with disapproval. Even out here, he had said, we could get someone on the run looking for a car. It wouldn't enhance his opinion of her when she took Kent's car, Sue admitted to herself with a sigh.

'Where's Clare?' Kent asked as he pulled off his jersey. 'I'll leave this, I don't need it now.' He threw the garment towards the bed, but it fell to the floor in a heap.

'Clare isn't up yet and—really, Kent! You are the limit! The only things you look after are those cameras of yours. Look at that garment!'

'I'd look after you,' he teased, his eyes laughing. 'Come on, darling, a kiss before parting?'

She fended him off lightly. 'Down, Fido! Down!'

'Time is on my side,' he said comfortably. He went off, grinning, and she watched him stride out into the brilliant clear day.

He may not be so happy when I see him next, Sue thought. He'll be angry. She hesitated, about to call to him and ask for the use of the car, but faltered. It would be no use. He would say amiably, 'I'll take you, Sue, no worries. You rest today——' Meanwhile time was passing, and every day added to the difficulty of getting to her destination.

She had not paused to work out all the problems, but the main thing was to go. She waited for a while before she opened the screen door and entered Kent's bedroom.

Automatically she picked up and folded the knitted jersey and put it on the bed. Her hand went to the keys and she had lifted them when Clare passed the door. Guilt made Sue start and she fumbled and almost dropped them.

'What on earth are you doing?' Clare asked, staring in at her.

'I—just folding Kent's jersey. He's hopeless—flung on the floor——'

'Why worry about his clothes? He's beyond reforming, you may as well realise it.'

'Just folded it,' Sue muttered again, and came out to the verandah.

106

Clare wore the red slack suit which was so smart, and had a scarf of emerald and red tucked in at the throat. She looked very groomed and elegant.

'Are you going to the yards?' Sue asked.

'Indeed, no! In these clothes?' Clare's face grew sullen. 'What on earth is there to do all day?'

Keys palmed in her hand, Sue stood listening, one part of her mind on the conversation, the other dismayed that Clare was in need of entertainment. A mobile, bored Clare could be a nuisance, for she needed company and conversation.

'I thought I might go,' lied Sue, 'later.' Don't let her decide to come, she thought.

'Oh, blast!' Clare fumed, 'I'll be here alone. I hate that.'

'Weren't you ever alone at home?' enquired Sue.

'With darling Mummy? She never goes out. I'd be so bored I'd be screaming.'

'Why didn't you work?'

'Why should I? Daddy is a wealthy man. I spent six months each year with him—why should I have to take a job?'

Sue shrugged. 'It would be more interesting.'

'Daddy leads a very social life. Too social, if you know what I mean, as far as women are concerned. He hadn't been so stupid,' Clare said bitterly, 'as to marry one of them before.'

She moved towards the edge of the verandah. Honeyeaters darted into the blossom on a shrub, but they did not interest her. She stared past them and, again, Sue had the irrational pity for her. She's had a rotten life, she thought, despite the money. Poor Clare...

The keys were hard and cold. Sue tried to say something, but her mind had become a blank. The choice was not a social one, of staying to keep Clare company or going to

107

join the others at the yards. She could not have Clare with her!

She shook her head, trying to clear it, and the other girl pushed her fingers into the pocket of her slack suit and pulled out a packet of cigarettes. She sauntered towards a canvas chair and snapped her lighter to flame.

'Talk to me! I'll have a cigarette and then I'll have a sleep to pass the time, after that woman brings the appalling stuff she calls coffee. "Smoke-oh", she calls the tea break! These bush phrases!'

'I rather like it,' Sue admitted, seating herself on the edge of a chair. 'I like the bush names.'

'You would!' Clare's glance was sardonic. 'You look as if you want to get up and go.'

Sue forced herself to relax and sit back. 'No, not yet. I may go and see the work later.'

'Who are you trying to impress?' Clare demanded.

She was cool. 'Nobody is interested in what I think of Yurla, Clare.'

'No. It's Undara you're trying to get hold of, isn't it?'

She had not realised that Clare knew so much, but why wouldn't she? Nick had talked, and after all, she was involved in Rory's life and interests.

Her petulant sniping freed Sue from her feeling of obligation. She got to her feet. 'My company isn't entertaining for you, Clare, is it? I'll go.'

Clare's lips were tight as she watched her leave the verandah. Sue went to the kitchen and the aboriginal girl made her a packet of sandwiches and a thermos of tea. The strips of plastic at the door, which kept flies at bay, rattled in the slight breeze. 'It's a nice day for an outing, Miss Howard,' the girl said cheerfully.

'Lovely.' Sue had to agree and smile happily, as though a morning out with the station work was the only thing on her mind.

She went to say goodbye to Clare, but she had gone from the verandah, and a few more minutes were wasted searching for her through the big house. Sue found her coming from the bathroom and inspecting a chip on the enamel of a fingernail. 'I'll see you later, Clare,' she said.

'Why not?' Clare retorted. 'There's nowhere else to be, is there?'

Sue was aware that the dark-haired girl stared after her speculatively. Surely I don't look guilty? she wondered. Does she suspect that I'm planning something?

She walked past the slim brown trunks of white cedars where seeds hung in gold clusters. A date palm rattled dryly in the breeze and the pet kangaroo sheltered in the shade of a kurrajong tree outside the fence. She made herself stroll casually towards the outbuildings; Sim Colter had gone, but she saw Frank's heavy back as he walked ponderously over a rise towards the vegetable garden.

At the shed she stood beside the big car and opened the door with secretive care. She slid into the driving seat and placed her hat beside her. The key was ready in her hand. Kent would be furious with her, she thought numbly, but it did not deter her. She could not allow it to stop her. Determination was like ice in her veins.

I'm going, she told herself. Nobody here has the right to stop me, or question me, except Rory.

The engine sounded very loud under the roof and she backed the vehicle out carefully and chose the track which headed west. Would Marj notice that she had taken the road which leads away from the yards?

After a while she passed the airstrip. There were white markers and a wind-sock, and YURLA was spelt out in white-painted stones. In time she came to the first bore and windmill where cockatoos were white blossoms on the steel lattice of the tower and about the water-trough, then emus stood motionless on the horizon as she drove through a

109

wheat-coloured sea of dried spinifex. The track was easy to follow. Under the tyres the sand produced a singing sound and Sue's spirits began to rise.

The road was like a trough between the well-reeded spinifex and red sand of the paddock. The country changed gradually and she drove out to open plains where mirage floated the sandhills like space-ships between earth and sky. Vaporous flecks of cloud drifted across the blue and the plain was shadeless, flat and empty, covered by tough, tenacious grasses and small scrub. It was a relief to come to the twisted hakeas and the dark foliage of native bauhinias.

She drove steadily, carefully, and the time sped by. She knew she should not think of Rory, but her mind knew no other thought. When he had spoken of her uncle's death he had asked bitterly, 'And if I was responsible? What then?'

Had there been sorrow in his voice? Or did he feel that he was above the law, that he could not be touched whatever he told her? Had there been cruel mockery in the half-confession to her, knowing that she had no witnesses?

That he won immense loyalty from those about him was very clear. Who would believe her, Sue asked herself, if she taxed him with his words? He would deny them.

The air grew hotter, but there was an unpolluted freshness about it and Sue could smell the honeyed sweetness of a hardy flowering tree. She drew in a deep breath and her confidence returned momentarily.

There must be a staff at Undara, she thought. I'll see them alone. It will be no conducted tour under Rory's supervision and with Kent hovering anxiously, loyal to his friend.

She had begun to realise that Rory was too powerful for her. She couldn't fight him.

She drove on into featureless, desolate kilometres and wondered at settlers taking up land in the area. There must have been bountiful rains and good seasons to lure them here. Had drought forced them out, in the end?

Sand patches received the weight of the vehicle with soft sinkings, and she had to concentrate nervously on driving the heavy car. Pale salmon-coloured sandhills fringed the horizon again and lines of saltbush and spinifex. When she came to the second bore it was a shock to see that the windmill was dismantled. There was an empty tank and a dry trough set on bare earth. The supply of water had failed. The track led past it, as Kent had described.

There was no focal point to the landscape. It rolled away, hard, dry, a stubbled grey expanse to all points of the compass. Cloud shadows patched the plain. The sun was overhead and Sue lost all sense of direction; there was the track, and she followed it blindly.

The morning passed and it was a relief to come to a fence line, to the stunted timber used for posts, to the metal gate and the name of the property on a faded board.

Undara.

Her first pulse of excitement changed to dismay. How desolate ... how lonely! Was this what Uncle Bryden had worked for, this arid area of land? She drove across a steel grid set as a barrier to stock and went on her way. It was no use getting agitated about the wisdom of her visit now. She was on Undara, and must continue.

It was on this desert stretch that she saw the grave beside the road. An isolated stone with just a name, any date or identification had been erased by years of blowing abrasive sand. A reminder of the early days of pioneering.

A sharp chill ran up her spine. This is what this country can do! This country I'm tackling so lightly ... She blinked at the dazzling sky and felt the slide of her sweating hands on the wheel. I must stop and eat, she thought, I'll feel better then. The lunch which had been packed for

111

her lay on the seat. She drove until there was timber again, with low-set cassias, flowering hakeas and thin-trunked mulga, sparse in foliage. There was no tree tall enough for shade and the thought of eating in the heated interior of the car did not tempt her.

At last, far away, she saw a windmill above the trees. Galahs were like roses set on the drab mulga about the bore, and water flowed from the pipe into a fenced, earth-walled tank set high above the ground level. From there it was piped to the troughs where several grey donkeys stood prick-eared, at her approach.

Sue ate the sandwiches there and strolled round while she sipped her tea. The screeching of the myriads of parrots was overwhelming. The donkeys trotted off.

She felt stronger and calmer after the break, tipped out the remains of the tea and walked briskly around the environs of the bore to ease the stiffness from her limbs. Then she set off again.

It was worrying when the surface changed and she could no longer see the wheel-tracks. She crashed over stones to a dry creek-bed and to large areas of shaly rock. When she won through to sandy soil again she was worried lest she might have lost her way.

Here, beside a dead tree, was the burnt-out shell of a car. The sun slid westward and slanted slightly, so that the remains of a big vehicle cast a black shadow on the red sand. Sue let the car slow down and frowned at the derelict wreck. The marks of fire-blackening were still visible but, in the dry air, rusting was a slow process. It was difficult for her to tell if the fire had been recent or if the wreck had been there for a long time.

Something vibrated along her nerves like a responsive chord, and she stopped the car and turned off the engine. It was as though all sound had died. Silence became a living entity about her.

Fear seeped into her for some reason she could not define; it was as though she absorbed an emotion from the air about her. Like an animal some primitive instinct alerted her and she stared at the motionless, battered shell as though it held a warning. Her eyes stared and her ears strained, trying to see beyond what was there to what it might have been, trying to hear beyond the nothingness which buzzed in her ears.

As her senses sharpened she heard small sounds, the hiss of sliding sand, the grating of a branch on a branch, a rattle of dry bark and a small buzz of an insect. She was shaking when she started the car and drove on, eyes slitted behind her sunglasses and her face tense.

It was bad country with black, shiny outcrops, ridges and dips, changing to bull-dust under the wheels so that the vehicle veered from side to side, sliding, skidding and in danger of bogging down. She urged the car as though it had been a willing horse. A flock of emus ran ahead of her, their feather-duster tails bobbing and ungainly in rapid movement.

The needle of the petrol gauge was showing empty: she must refill the tank from Kent's jerrycans. It was a heavy job and she had hoped not to do it, had hoped the petrol in the tank might be sufficient for the distance.

She was weaker physically than she had admitted, and her head ached. A glance at her watch told her that time was passing and the afternoon was slipping away.

She stumbled as she got out to stand beside the vehicle and the heat of the metal body overwhelmed her. She opened the boot and leaned in to lift a can, bracing herself for the weight. One hand fumbled for the strainer, plastic-wrapped, which she had seen Kent use when replacing fuel in dusty conditions on the track.

She was regretting that she had come; all the early resolution flickered and faded. What an infernal cheek she

113

had, taking the car, presuming on Kent's affection and understanding. He had asked her to wait until he could come with her, until Rory would arrange a visit.

It came back to Rory each time...

Sue's breath whistled out in a sound like a sob and her movements were arrested suddenly as though frozen. She was clamped in the position she held, her legs powerless, her arm outstretched to the fuel can.

It had lifted easily. Weightless ... Empty ...

She pushed her body further into the boot and leaned over to fumble at the other khaki-coloured cans. They clashed together and her fingers were curled tight on the metal handles. She was cold, cold in the sweltering heat.

The cans were empty.

In dumb horror she saw her own hand go to the water container, but knew as she did so that there was no liquid behind the walls of the can.

Her blouse was soaked with sweat, the sweat of heat and fright. Somebody had emptied out the life-giving water and poured out the petrol, or substituted other cans that were empty. She noticed the sacking tucked between them so that the rattle would not alert her. She straightened and stood, slight and pale, and tried to fight back her panic.

There was no way the cans could have been emptied by accident! She closed her eyes, remembering Kent sketching the map in the sand at the entrance to the shed. They had walked away and left it for anyone to see.

Anyone? She could see, in retrospect, the man who had worked, or pretended to, at the back of the building while she talked to Kent. Their voices—had they carried clearly to him as he moved about his task? Had he listened, Sim Colter, the man who worked on Undara? Had he been the one to act swiftly when he realised that she intended to use the car?

She had not been able to talk to him at the muster, but she recalled his appearance, quick in movement about the fire which his mother had situated in isolation, a thin, tough bushman wearing a wide-brimmed felt hat which hid his eyes. A straight, hard mouth.

Mrs Colter's son . . .

She started the motor and began to drive. It was the only thing to do. Action would ease her shivers of fright. She must drive while there was fuel in the tank, then she must wait for somebody to come.

She knew enough of the conditions out here not to risk walking unless the way and distance were known—Kent had outlined the precautions in one of his informative talks.

Never leave the vehicle, he had said forcibly. There's water in the radiator that may save your life, if you're desperate. Besides, he had added, in this immensity of countryside a human being is a dot of nothing from the air. If they're searching for you, a car they *can* see!

She was to have the humiliation of being rescued, rescued by Rory, whom she had tried to evade, so she must accept it, try to carry it off with as much poise as she could muster and face him with her head high.

She did not know full terror or forget her brave decisions until she saw a larger shadow across the sand ahead, black, implacable and clear-cut. The ruins of the burned car!

She had doubled back on her tracks at some point and followed the pads where donkeys trod or pathways worn by sheep, instead of the faint, dust-obscured car tracks, and this was outback Australia where people died of dehydration and exposure.

In that paralysed moment she knew she had taken the situation too lightly. She wondered if anyone would know that she had come to Undara. She had lied to the girl in the kitchen and told her she was to follow Kent to the yards;

115

out where the men were working they thought she was safely at the homestead. When it was found that she was missing it might be assumed that she had mistaken the road to the yards and driven on eastwards.

Would they think to look for her in this direction?

The picture was complete in her mind in one shaft of crushing nightmare reality.

Was she to die out here, alone, with so much distance between her and the homestead at Yurla that she could not attempt to walk there, and with Undara house an unknown distance ahead of her? She had underestimated the hatred of her adversary. She sat, taut, staring through the dusty windscreen and her small face grew determined. I shall not accept this, she decided grimly. Kent will miss me. He'll guess that I've come to Undara. Nick may return, perhaps, and insist on a search.

She drew a long breath. First she would drive away from this wreck. It had a haunting effect, somehow. The petrol would run out soon ...

When she had to stop she placed her thick jersey ready for the cooler hours ahead. She searched the car and pulled the sacking from beneath the cans. Rough covering, but better than nothing. Another lesson notched up—throwing out the tea had been recklessness and folly.

She schooled herself to endurance, to patience, and to control her wildly imaginative thoughts. The sun grew red and slipped down the sky into the glory of clouds tinted scarlet and gold.

She could not see beyond the next few hours. They had to be lived through first. As the sky darkened a storm began to gather on the south-western horizon. Intermittent lightning flared against the low mass of grey clouds: a dry storm which produced no rain.

She sat out the brief twilight and the early hours of dark-

116

ness and had not thought to sleep. The moon was white and rounded above twisted boughs when she heard somebody trying to open the door.

She woke with a start and could see Rory's rugged face, the strong hair above the forehead, the wide shoulders against the brilliant light. She shook herself free of the covering and sat up.

'Oh, it's you,' she said icily.

'My God!' he exclaimed. 'You look for trouble! What in heaven's name do you think you're doing?'

'Going to Undara,' she said curtly, and got out to stand in front of him. She was shaken to realise that he had driven up and she had heard nothing, nor seen the lights of his vehicle.

His big hands clamped on her shoulders and were hard and merciless. She could see that his face was strained and the anger in his eyes. 'I told you I would take you to Undara! Couldn't you wait?'

Sue could feel the jerk of her heart and said in stark bitterness, 'I was afraid, I think.'

'Afraid—of me?' His grip loosened.

'The tree branch—the cattle——' she muttered.

His arms dropped to his sides. 'We'll camp here,' he said flatly. 'I've had a long day in the yards and don't intend to drive all night, as well.'

She watched while he piled thin twigs and dry grass together and the butt ends of old trees to be added later. He boiled the billy and they drank tea in silence, then he flung a bedroll on the ground.

'Use that,' he snapped.

'It's yours,' she faltered.

'I'll use another blanket that's in the vehicle.' He looked down at her and added cuttingly, 'Surely you don't have to be difficult about every little thing!'

She curled up in the warmth of the blankets, conscious of his motionless figure on the other side of the fire. Red glare danced on the low trees and the chill of the night was about them, and the silence. The silence. There was no way Sue could break it.

How had she come to suspect Rory so deeply? Was it Nick's attitude which had influenced her? Or did she, in some extraordinary way, have to be different from Clare who had returned from abroad to be with him? Did she want to be noticed?

There was an element of it in their relationship, she had to admit, but there was more behind it. The mystery of Undara and her uncle's death stood between them. He had been there when Uncle Dryden died. He had said so, and he had hinted at blame...

A falcon soared high above them as the daylight tinted the eastern sky. Shivering in the blankets, Sue watched Rory, bulky in his heavy jacket, as he pushed the sticks together and coaxed the coals to flame.

He felt her eyes on him and his mouth was a grim line when he spoke. If you trust me to offer you food——'

She shrugged. 'Don't be ridiculous.' She came to stand at the fire, holding her hands to the warmth. 'You've prospered. Why didn't Uncle Dryden? Was it the drinking?'

'Who said he was a poor man?' he demanded. 'He wasn't a drunkard, either. He could hold his liquor.' He waved to the country about them. 'He had hard country, as you can see for yourself.'

'Why did he come here?' she asked, bewildered. 'Why did he stay?'

'He loved the Outback. Isn't that a good enough reason to live here?' He handed her a plate of hot foot and she accepted it gratefully.

'You're prepared for all eventualities, it seems,' she said as she ate.

'And you aren't. Why are you marooned here?'

She paused and her voice was sober. 'It's not my choice. Did you think it was?'

Rory flicked an end of burning wood into the fire and began to push sand over it with his boot. 'That damned car of Kent's let you down, did it? You'd have done better to pinch one of my vehicles, wouldn't you?'

'The spare fuel was tipped out or the cans replaced with empties, and so was the water,' she answered starkly.

He stood quite still and it was a while before he lifted his head. She met his eyes with a level look.

His voice had changed. 'So you were stranded in a more serious fashion. I thought you'd run out of petrol.'

'And hadn't the brains to do anything about it? I do observe, and I want to learn. I could have driven to Undara if there had been extra fuel, as there had been. Kent had checked, I saw it done.' Some mad impulse made her add flippantly, 'I can't suspect you of the changeover, as you weren't at home.'

'I'd been back to the shed,' he said, thin-lipped, 'didn't you know that I drove back to check some stock figures at the office? Kent and I went out in the Land Rover with Sim.'

Sue felt giddy. It had been an idiotic thing to say, a half-gesture of trust which had gone wrong. Why, in her folly, must she keep pricking him?

His voice held no inflection. 'We'll talk at Undara.'

He tipped the dregs of tea over the covered fire, and with brisk movements produced petrol from the Land Rover and got the car going for her. Then he drove ahead and she followed in Kent's car.

Her first glimpse of Undara was of a collection of roofs, a

cluster of pale shapes with brown, lightly timbered country stretching far away in all directions with the red ridges of sandhills breaking the horizon here and there. There was a tufting of grey-green about the buildings which were dwarfed in the immensity, and mirages shimmered about the sandhills.

At the grid to another paddock Rory dropped back and she drove up beside him. 'There's your uncle's home,' he said.

She said hoarsely, 'It's very isolated, isn't it?'

It had been impossible to picture isolation such as this; it was beyond her experience and knowledge. Her mind was filled with questions about the man who had lived here. How had he faced the solitude? Had the drinking been a solace in the life he led?

There were vast spaces of gibber and weed and scattered ghost gums, white as chalk against brown soil.

They passed a turkey's nest tank, set above the earth and resembling the incubation mound made by the native bird. Here a windmill pumped water from hidden sources far below the surface. Rory frowned and let his vehicle slow to a halt.

Water had spread into the ground about the trough, and a flock of wild green budgerigars swirled aloft on green arcs of wings, shrilling and calling, from the soak. They came to rest in a stark, lifeless tree and the bare branches burgeoned in green again with the vivid bodies of hundreds of birds. Sue had halted, too, and cried out admiringly. Rory was out studying the seepage and he smiled briefly, enmity forgotten.

'They're beautiful in their natural element, aren't they? You realise that water is wasting? I'll take you to the house and return to check what's wrong. It's far too precious to run away in that fashion.'

The house and garden were hidden by a high fence of galvanised iron which Sue thought very ugly. Why not timber? Lack of it, she supposed, in the country of puny trees. When she saw the sand whipped into tiny ripples by the breeze she realised that there could be sound reason for the barrier. On the roof, visible over the fence, 'Undara' was painted in white against what had once been green.

It gave her a strange feeling. It had meant so much to her unknown uncle, it seemed, yet her mother had kept the invitation secret from them until she was dying. There was a large woolshed a distance away, and other outbuildings which Sue was too agitated to notice in the first moments.

Rory stopped the Land Rover and came back to open the door of the car. 'What do you think of it?' he asked coldly.

She could not answer. Athel trees topped the fence; she could see the drooping grey-green foliage. There were groves of the same trees about the other buildings, but the countryside was so vast and overpowering that she felt the trees were pitiful and inadequate to soften the harsh surroundings.

Why hadn't she stayed in England? It was lonely without Nick here, alone with Rory and his politeness, and the questions not answered.

She had come so far, stubbornly, in the face of opposition to find the place, but was shaken by a terrible reluctance to enter the high-walled enclosure of the garden.

CHAPTER SIX

'COME in,' urged Rory. 'We'll have a cup of tea and I'll go and fix the bore. A man from the outstation was here while the Colters have been at Yurla, but he went back to his work this morning.'

'How do you know?' Sue asked, surprised.

'The radio-transceiver,' he replied.

What a fool she had been to have forgotten that! He could have contacted Undara long before she had arrived and alerted them that she was coming!

She got out slowly and felt the sand yield under her feet, felt the warmth of the sun and screwed her eyes shut against the glare.

He opened a gate, also of galvanised iron, and led her through. There were portable gas cylinders lined up against a wall and hot water pipes were lagged, she was fascinated to notice, with strips of hairy green hide. Around the trees were deep pits and she could see houses lying about the garden. There was an extremely large tank in the garden enclosure, set higher than the house, and a windmill turned lazily beside it.

She looked about her as she walked slowly towards the house. There was a verandah at the front and the side walls were windowed here and there with shades over the glass. The timber was painted a creamy colour and the boards had a weathered look.

Rory swung the door open at the top of three wide and shallow steps, and they entered directly into the back of the house in the informality of the bush.

The room was used for dining and was large. A big polished table was set about by eight plain chairs; windows looked to the back garden where Sue saw a wire-netted trellis covered by a prickly rambling rose covered in yellow flowers. Beyond it were other buildings which she observed briefly.

Rory gestured to the left. 'The kitchen.' He glanced at his watch. 'I'll put the kettle on.'

She followed him to the plain room. There was good equipment and the room was clean but had no frills. A man's home.

She felt confused and in the way as she watched Rory light the gas jet and fill a kettle. He opened cupboards and produced cake tins and biscuits, then swiftly sliced a large, moist fruit cake. 'Mrs Colter is a good cook.' He looked at her measuringly. 'She'll be back tonight, so you won't be alone here.'

'You must feel angry with me,' she muttered. 'I realise I must be an awful pest. Can you see my side of it at all?'

'Haring out here from England, irresponsibly, to an uncle of whom you know nothing?'

Her smile was bitter. 'If you must phrase it like that——'

Rory found a tin of preserved milk and opened it to add to their tea and they carried their pottery mugs to the big table. He sat with his back to the inner wall and she sat opposite. He seemed so competent and at ease that she felt her awkwardness deepen. 'I thought it was for the best,' she faltered.

'I'm afraid it isn't.' A fly, trapped, buzzed inside the glass behind her and he got up to throw the window wide. He changed the subject. 'There's no air-conditioning here, but you shouldn't find the heat too unbearable. It isn't summer.'

'You have air-conditioning at Yurla,' Sue pointed out.

'Your uncle was an outdoors man and had few guests.'

The cake was extremely good and the tea refreshing, and she ate and drank in silence for a few minutes. Then, in a burst of honesty, she spoke quickly.

'It's no use, I can't fight you, Rory. I shouldn't have brought Nick out here.'

'What mischief had he been in?' he questioned.

She coloured hotly. 'Mischief?'

'Was it you, then?' A dark eyebrow lifted sardonically.

'It was Nick. He was running round with a wild gang——'

He said caustically, 'Any reform has to come from him, not from your efforts to change him.'

She put her mug down quickly and her eyes were troubled.

He added, 'I gather, from what Kent has told me, that you two are alone in the world.'

Alone in the world. It had a sinister sound and she did not like the phrase. 'We have friends,' she said quickly.

He said shortly, aware in an instant of her unease, 'I won't kill you here and bury you in the garden, Sue.'

She jerked her head up and stared at him. 'Oh, let's stop fencing! Nick had been up before a magistrate. He was with youths who were caught stealing, and he was very fortunate to be cleared of taking part. That was why my mother was so keen to get him away, to begin a new life. The city would have destroyed him. He was too idle, too bored.'

Rory sat quietly while she told him of the escapades in which her brother had been involved and it did not seem a strange thing that she should be confiding in him, after all that had happened between them.

'To come to Australia might have been sound,' he admitted, 'if you'd planned it better.'

'I thought it *was* planned, or partly so. My mother was

124

ill, of course, and her thoughts weren't clear——' she added firmly, 'in any case, we were prepared to stay in Brisbane and work if he didn't want us. We didn't hear from him and Kent offered to bring us out. So we came to see what would come of it.'

'Then you heard that he'd been killed?' he enquired.

She took a deep breath. 'Yes, on the way.'

'So, breathing revenge, you came charging in on me——'

'We came to you to try and find out what had happened and where we stand!' Her nerves grew taut again. Rory did not answer her challenge but rose quickly.

'I'll go and look at the trough. Go into the house, if you like. The inner rooms are unlocked.'

After he had gone Sue opened the door to the living room. The radio-transceiver was set beside a window and there was an old-fashioned, glass-fronted bookcase filled with books. The armchairs were leather-covered and the couch, and a round table carried some polished stones. Uncurtained windows, shining timber floors and no mats. The dust, of course . . .

No frills because of the dust, but—how bare! Yet there was a certain charm in the austerity and severity of the room and furnishing.

There were three bedrooms and the wooden walls were the same clean ivory colour throughout. In each room was a bed covered by cotton bedspreads, chests of drawers and built-in wardrobes. A bathroom was set behind the bedrooms and a passage led to the front verandah.

Sue walked out to the weathered boards of the floor and noted the desiccated dryness of the timber. Trees had been planted close to the verandah and the leaves gave an illusion of coolness as sun filtered through greenery. She went down the steps to the golden sandy soil of the garden, and it was as though a shadowy figure went with her. He

125

must have trodden this way, have used these steps, this path—her unknown uncle.

The garden was hot, lizard-haunted, gay with flowers, white daisies with blue centres, geraniums brilliant in colour, succulents and cacti. There were magnificent roses on tall bushes, which surprised her, for she had not expected to see familiar blossoms in this place. Her uncle's pleasure, the garden? Or Mrs Colter's work?

In the tangled branches of the rambling rose on the trellis the orange-beaked zebra finches, with their striped tails, trilled their quaint song; Sue saw several grass nests in the thorny security. Beneath the trellis was a bed of beautiful violets, and she bent her head, shaken by a longing for England and English gardens. The delicate and beautiful scent was all about her.

She came to a large laundry, roofed with canegrass, with set-in tubs and a washing machine. The iron-roofed shed next to it housed a well-oiled and shining engine and banks of batteries. Sue realised that this was where the power was generated for lighting and equipment. Behind this, beyond a grove of Parkinsonia trees, spiny, yellow-flowered, was a neat white cottage, vine-hung, windows closed and doors shut.

She turned away. If this was where Mrs Colter lived with her son it might be wisest not to trespass until invited. If I'm invited, she thought, if I stay . . . This stolen glimpse might be all she was allowed of Undara.

Rory drove back in a cloud of dust at lunch-time and strode into the house. Sue had found a large slab of cold roast meat in the refrigerator and there were tinned salads. He nodded when he saw her preparations.

'I've struck trouble at the bore. Repairs will take some time.'

'I can manage here,' she replied.

They did not talk while they ate. What can I say to him? Sue reflected desperately, conscious of the silence. The tree branch ... the cattle ... his pretended lack of knowledge of the reason for her being stranded could have been a poor cover. He had followed with little time wasted. He had known she would be there, and now she was alone at Undara with him.

He was the only one who had a motive to harm them, or scare them off. She said in a taut, strung-up voice, 'Tell me how you acquired Undara, Rory.'

'I'll do it,' he said harshly, 'but, for God's sake, not over the lunch table and with the bore spilling water everywhere.'

She grabbed the dishes and carried them to the sink with fingers that had lost strength suddenly. 'It will be in your good time, then!'

He was forceful as he grabbed his hat and strode down the steps, ruled by a black rage. Sue walked through the house again and found her small valise on one of the beds. When had it been placed there? Had Rory brought it, packed for her needs? She opened it and her lips firmed. One change of clothing could not mean a lengthy stay!

She could not rest. She took up her shady cloth hat and put on her sun-glasses and went out into the garden again. Rory had been efficient in his movements. The hoses trickled in pits at the bases of trees and finches dipped their beaks in the runnels of water.

It seemed a touching gesture, keeping a dead man's garden green. Or keeping an asset in good order?

She must not let herself be stupid about Rory. She must try and assess things coolly. At the moment he loomed over-large in her mind and, with bitter self-knowledge, she admitted that it had been so since she met him.

She went from one outbuilding to another and saw old

127

vehicles, harness and machinery. At the back of a shed was a waggon, decayed and weather-worn, and beneath it piles of collars, hames and the leather of harness, stiff as iron in the dry air. She saw the workshop and a large woolshed where the sheep were shorn, and big yards enclosed hoof-trodden earth which had set hard. There were shearer's quarters and a utility truck stood in another building, but there was no car. Surely Uncle Dryden had had a car? Would Rory have taken it, sold it, perhaps?

She could see in retrospect the burnt-out shell on the track. The car that had been destroyed by fire.

I'll ask Rory, she thought. I'll ask about that. She knew in her heart that there was some story about the car, and that it tied in with their own links with Undara.

The heat reflected from the ground and stones shimmered in the sun. The horizon was empty of life. The sky was a vast clean bowl above her as she looked up and turned about slowly. She felt diminished and tiny, of no consequence to the country. I could go, and it will be the same, she realised, and has been the same for aeons and aeons of time.

Whether it was the turning around or the thought, she felt dizzy again. The country was implacable, harsh. She walked on, head up, drawing deep breaths of the pure air. Had Uncle Dryden loved it, this hard country, or had he failed to measure up? Was that why he earned the name Brandy?

A sandhill had covered a fence in the distance and she walked towards it. It was further than she imagined in the deceptive countryside with few large vertical objects to give perspective. A new length of fence had been placed on top of the dune and above the buried section. She climbed the sand wall and red grains slid under her feet and filled her shoes. There was a group of trees beyond the dune, and a building half buried in sand, interest quickened as she slipped and slid down the sand-face towards it.

The walls were of mud and straw, hard-puddled and packed. A pisé house! The roof was gone, and weather had eroded the clay without its protection. There was a separate room, cane-grass walled, with rusty roofing iron still in place. At one end was a rough-set stone fireplace and Sue, stepping over a fallen beam to enter the doorway, saw remains of metal there, indicating that a stove had filled the square opening below the rattling iron chimney.

It's a wonder the cook didn't set the walls alight, she thought, touching the brittle, tinder-dry straw held in place by layers of twisted wires. All the metal was rusted and eroded, so it must have stood through some wet seasons as well as many dry ones. Red sand poured through an aperture which had once been covered by a wooden shutter.

The roofless rooms of the house were bare and stones and a few bottles lay on the stone floor. Here, too, sand drifted through breaks in the walls.

A deserted house is a melancholy thing and Sue looked about, lips parted, picturing it as it might have been. Was this the home to which her uncle came after he left England? Had he lived here until he built the bigger house? In the talks at Yurla she had heard references to the distances, the cost of transporting goods from the cities, and had begun to realise that the simplest dwelling could be costly to provide.

He must have worked on other properties, 'getting experience', they called it. 'I got my experience on Wattle Creek', she had heard one of the men say. Uncle Dryden had learned how to run a property and then came to this corner of Australia, arid, inhospitable, and remote, and buried himself here at Undara. She felt a sudden and overwhelming certainty that his exile had been a self-imposed one.

Why did you come here, Uncle Dryden? Why did you stay? How did you die?

The sand gave way to brown earth and a vast open area which appeared to be a dried bed of an ancient lake. In the mass of reedy grass Sue saw several large kangaroos, uncaring of her presence. She stood and watched and heard the sheep begin to bleat loudly as they moved away.

A man walked below her towards the trough; lean, capable, and quick-moving. His wide hat was down over his eyes and Sue studied him openly as he stood with his back towards her.

Sim Colter was back at Undara. What a good chance to have a few words with him, without his mother's chilling presence to inhibit them! She walked closer, her feet brushing the dead leaves and cracking the dry sticks under her shoes.

He stood squarely, his feet set apart in the narrow, elastic-sided riding boots and his thin legs slightly bowed. Even from the back one would know him to be a horseman, Sue thought fleetingly. She called to him, 'Hello, there!'

There was no response and she walked closer, feeling foolish. She could see sweat marks on his shirt and the way his dark hair grew on his neck and the stiff set of his shoulders. A slight man, but strong and tall.

'Oh, hello. I was walking——'

She jerked to a halt as he moved away from her with a purposeful and determined stride. His head did not turn and he did not look at her. She stood helplessly, and watched him walk away.

Defiance stiffened her dismay to anger. Her voice was raw and strident as she shouted. 'Hey! I want to talk to you. Wait a moment!'

Under her disbelieving gaze he passed from her view behind a wing of the sandhill. Her lips set tight. So! That was the way it was to be! They feared questioning, it would seem, Mrs Colter and her son. They were determined to avoid it.

We shall see, she promised herself. We shall see.

When she returned to the house Sue had a wash and brushed her hair, and she was glad she had tidied herself when she saw Clare come in at the gateway. Sue walked out into the garden to meet her.

Clare wore lavender slacks and shirt and had a scarf tied round her glossy dark hair in studied artistic casualness. She spoke with no attempt to be charming. 'What the hell are you playing at, Sue Howard? Getting Rory to run off after you and leave me flat at Yurla?'

Sue tried not to be antagonised by the tone. 'It was all a mistake, Clare.'

'A clever mistake,' Clare snapped, and her seething rage was obvious.

Sue was jolted, seeing the position from the other girl's angle. 'Everything was—all right. I mean, because we were out at night alone——' she faltered.

'You're a scheming little bitch,' Clare said coolly and clearly, not attempting to lower her voice.

'Oh, don't be so bloody-minded, Clare!' Kent said lazily from the gate. 'You sound like every enraged woman since time began! Sue wanted to get to Undara, and she came. After all, it was her uncle's home. Rory felt it his duty to be protective, that's all.'

'We had hoped to have a pleasant evening when Rory came home from the trucking,' she snapped.

'*You* had hoped to have a pleasant evening, dear girl,' he said crisply.

'Sue would have been there,' she argued, 'should have been there! You'd have been hanging around, too. We've had no chance to be alone.'

'We'd have absented ourselves tactfully once dinner was over.' Kent put his arm about Sue protectively. 'She'd asked me about borrowing the car. I knew she intended going.'

Sue could not bear that he should lie for her but, when she looked up quickly, he grinned down at her conspiringly and pressed her shoulder.

'Let it rest, Clare. Your jealousy isn't becoming.'

Sue wondered if Clare sensed that Rory's physical attraction was disturbing, and was wary of its effect on another girl. Why wouldn't she realise it? She loved him. She would know the appeal of his dark ruggedness.

Clare took a step away, but the atmosphere was heavy with her emotion. 'Why on earth have we had to come to this dump?' She looked about wildly and disparagingly. 'All I can say is, your uncle must have been out of his mind! The place is the absolute end!'

A peculiar sensation pervaded Sue's body; a stiffening of the spine, a prickle of resentment, and a flare of pride. Loyalty, that was the word to describe it. She felt loyalty and a rush of protective fury. 'It's plain but it's comfortable, Clare,' she said stiffly.

She bit back more words. It was no longer her uncle's home, the house was Rory's. This girl was to be his wife and the house would belong to her as well. It was a dismaying thought.

As Kent had been able to come upon them unheard on the soft earth, so Rory appeared and Clare, knowing he had heard her remark, added quickly a light and amused comment.

'I'll be in worse surroundings than these from time to

time as I move about the country with you, Rory.' She hid her feelings, with practised ease, and went over to rub a smooth cheek on his shoulder. 'I'm being niggly! All the driving and dust——! I'm tired. What about a drink, Rory?'

'Mrs Colter has arrived and is in the kitchen preparing dinner. We'll have our drinks on the verandah. Come on, Clare, let's get them.'

Sue moved within Kent's grasp and he drew her closer. She felt a tight, knotted discomfort in her inside. We're in neat pairs, she thought. Clare and Rory. Sue and Kent ...

She was brusque. 'I'm sorry, Kent. I'm not in the mood.'

He smoothed her hair with one long-fingered hand and tried to kiss her, but she evaded him lightly and laughed so that he would not be too serious, 'Too much too soon for me, Kent. All this huge country overwhelming me, and Nick in hospital in a town I don't even know——'

'He'll be out tomorrow. That's the last report,' he told her.

Sue showered and changed before dinner and smiled sourly as she donned the slack suit that had been packed for her. By Marj Settler, perhaps——? A woman's touch was indicated by the fact that she had her toilet requisites. She rinsed out her jeans and blouse and underclothes, knowing they would be dry an hour after she hung them on the clothes line beside the laundry, then walked round the outside of the house and joined the others on the verandah. Both men rose from the big canvas chairs as she came up the steps.

Rory poured her a drink and brought it to her. She caught a glimpse of the expression in his eyes and it puzzled her. He looks as though I've wounded him in some way, she thought. I can't understand him. If I had no doubts about Uncle Dryden's affairs, could we have been

133

friends? No, not then, either. Friends? There was something too explosive between them for mild friendship.

She sipped her drink and listened to Clare describing an evening in Paris at the night clubs.

'Won't you miss it, Clare?' Kent asked idly.

Clare smiled, a secret, confident smile. 'I don't expect to.'

It was an ambiguous statement, but nobody followed it up. Sue plunged into the pause with her own query.

'What's the matter with Sim Colter? He's very unfriendly, isn't he? I gave him a hail today and he ignored me.'

She laid it on the line deliberately, in front of them all. Rory could not refuse to answer while the others listened. He frowned at her and seemed as though he would speak, but Kent broke in quickly. 'Good lord, Sue, hadn't you realised? It didn't occur to me that you didn't know.'

'Know what?' It was not working out as she had hoped.

'He's a deaf mute.'

Numbly she stared at him and after a moment swung to face Rory.

He nodded. 'He was born that way. Mrs Colter came here to work when he was a boy and later your uncle took him on the payroll as a hand, helping round the place. Gradually Sim took on sheep work. He's very good with the sheep.'

'Isn't it a handicap to him?' Sue asked.

Clare said dismissingly, 'With people he lip-reads. Who wants to hear the bleating of sheep, anyway?'

Sue began to think of the situation presented by her fresh knowledge. Mrs Colter would cling to the safe niche for her son! She was startled by the information. Sim, too, would not want his life pattern disturbed by the young relatives from England who threatened to upset the arrangements at

Undara in which everyone had their place.

Rory left them and walked into the big room, and she heard his voice as he spoke over the radio transceiver. When he returned to join them he appeared withdrawn and aloof.

'Your brother is returning tomorrow,' he told Sue.

She braced herself, half dreading the impact of Nick's personality on the household. 'Is there a plane landing at Undara tomorrow?' she asked.

His lips firmed. 'Gerry Darker is flying him here.'

Clare straightened. 'How on earth does *he* come into it?'

'He has his ear to every whisper,' he said bitingly. 'He stopped off in town, contacted your brother at the hospital and arranged it.'

Sue wished he would not keep referring to Nick as 'your brother'.

'A perfect excuse to call at Undara,' Clare commented.

Kent's smile was lopsided and teasing as he glanced at Sue. 'Doesn't take these English beauties long to get our wealthy Gerry interested!' he joked.

Sue was embarrassed but lifted her chin. 'It's good of him to bring Nick.'

'Very good.' The dead level of Rory's voice was forbidding.

They went in to dinner. As the large leg of corned mutton was carved Sue stole a glance at Clare; the homely food would not be to her liking. In the centre of the table a small bowl was filled with some of the tiny banksia roses, and the white cloth set off the yellow of their colour. The unadorned silver was good but severely utilitarian. As she had thought before, it was obvious that it was a man's home, comfortable but unadorned by the touches which delight a woman. A house for use and not for luxury.

A house of smouldering secrets ...

135

When Nick arrived next day Kent drove Sue to meet the plane after it had buzzed the house.

Gerry was exuberant. 'I had to return this way. Such an excellent opportunity and a perfect excuse!' He glanced about appraisingly. He would not be able to look at country, or a woman, without the unconscious assessment in his eyes, Sue thought. She pretended not to see his well-kept, outstretched hand.

Nick grinned at her briefly. He seemed paler, thinner, in the few days of his absence.

'Was it bad, Nick?' she asked anxiously. 'Painful?'

'Not really.' He dismissed it and did not ask how she had fared, or if she had recovered. She did not expect it from him.

Gerry swung Nick's case down lightly and looked and tethered the plane before he got into the car.

'You should get some photos of my aircraft,' he said largely, 'might be money in it for you, Woodley, and help you along a bit. My news value, you know. You could sell them to a newspaper.'

Sue sensed that he had rubbed Kent on the raw and there was a cool silence.

'Where's Rory?' Nick asked.

'Out on the run. He took Sim Colter with him to an outstation,' Kent said briefly.

'Never a dull moment,' Nick commented dryly. There seemed to be a firmness to his mouth, a hint of resolution, and Sue looked at him quickly. He seemed to have become more mature and decisive.

'Rory will be back for lunch,' she said, 'he asked you to stay if you liked, Gerry.' The invitation had conveyed little warmth when it had been given and Sue did not infuse more into it when she passed it on.

Gerry leaned forward in the back seat so that his head was close beside Sue's where she sat beside Kent in the

136

front. If she turned suddenly her cheek must brush his. 'Naturally I'll stay,' he said, beside her ear, and with meaning in the tone.

Nick sat stiffly in the back corner, his plastered right wrist supported by a sling and his expression tense and patient, as though he was reserving his energies for a later occasion.

At the house there was a smell of fresh baking and Mrs Colter had wheeled a trolley to the front verandah and left it there, with the teacups set out and the cakes and scones ready to serve. Clare was out of bed and dressed, elegant in a simple woollen dress of dark green. She poured the tea, completely in command. Sue realised that it was on social occasions that the other girl was happiest and at her best.

Kent perched on the floor with his feet on the top step and stared out at the garden. The scones were hot and the cake rich with the goodness of new-laid eggs.

Gerry took a second piece and commented, 'She's a good cook, that woman you have,' to Clare, as though she were already mistress of the house.

'Do you think so?' she said disparagingly. 'She doesn't satisfy me, I'm afraid. These bush cooks have much to learn in the art of serving fine food.'

'Do you know a place in Sydney called the Red Coq?' he asked, eyes gleaming.

Mrs Colter came to the door with a jug of hot water and heard Clare's cutting remark. Her strong face was impassive but her eyes flashed. She placed the jug in front of Clare and walked out again. 'She heard you,' Sue said, distressed.

'So what?' Clare snapped. 'They're too casual. Your uncle was easy-going, evidently. Men alone become slovenly, I suppose.'

Gerry did not notice the exchange and broke in with another remark about a Cordon Bleu restaurant in Sydney which Clare knew. 'It's a wonder I haven't met you,' he said at last. 'We seem to haunt the same places.'

'I don't get many chances,' she said, with a twist to her lips, 'with my dear mum in the background. She's careful with the money, my mama!'

He chuckled, not taking her seriously, and smiled at Sue. 'I'll have to show you the sights of Sydney, Sue. You'll love it there. My home is right on the water on a cliff overlooking the harbour.'

'You don't spend much time there,' Kent observed.

'Enough,' he admitted cheerfully. 'I have a home in Switzerland, too. A very handy tax lurk, that one!'

'It would be,' Rory said dryly, from the door.

Clare went across and stood beside him. 'You're back early. I'm so glad.'

Talk became general and, after a while, Sue saw Nick rise and leave the group. She made an excuse and followed him. She found him in the garden staring at the glossy globes of oranges among the green leaves.

He turned and narrowed his eyes at her critically. 'You seem to be on a pretty friendly footing with Rory,' he observed.

She gasped. 'Friendly? Don't be silly, Nick!'

'Some party!' he said sourly. 'Sipping tea together, all good friends.'

She said bleakly, 'There's no chance of us being friends with Rory while the question of Undara isn't settled, Nick. We have to give him a chance to tell us the story.'

'He'll have his opportunity,' he said bitterly. 'He's taken long enough to do it.'

'We haven't given him a chance,' she admitted honestly, 'arriving in the middle of mustering.'

'I'll give him until tonight.' Nick was adamant. 'Then I'm flying to Sydney and I'll engage a private detective to

138

start an enquiry into Uncle Dryden's death and how Rory got his hands on the place.'

For some reason she protested, 'Don't rush into anything, Nick.'

'Rush? What do you call rush? You're a bit sold on him, Sue,' he jibed.

She coloured hotly. 'Of course I'm not!'

'Gerry said he'll be back tomorrow, and I can go to Sydney with him then. He'll take us both, Sue.'

'Back tomorrow?' she echoed.

'He's going on to another of his properties for tonight and will come back here tomorrow and pick us up.'

She had a terrible feeling of being swept away by his hasty arrangements and Gerry's forceful personality.

'We'll have to talk to Rory first,' she said feebly.

After Gerry had gone and Rory and Kent had gone out in the Land Rover, Nick walked to the sandhill. Clare had gone to her room to read and rest and the house grew quiet.

Sue went through the garden and knocked on the door of the white cottage. In her own neat home Mrs Colter seemed less formidable and more feminine, though the dress she wore was a plain one with the severe lines of a uniform. Her crisp, greying hair was short and stood out in its own firm waves around her beaky face. She opened the door wide. 'I thought you'd be coming.'

Sue admired her dignity and felt an intruder as she entered the small, comfortably furnished sitting room with the brick fireplace, filled now by a spreading green fern. Here, as in the big house, was the same lack of unnecessary objects and the same sense of space was achieved. However, there were white nylon curtains at the windows. Mrs Colter was a woman whom dust would not defeat.

'I want to talk about my uncle,' Sue said firmly.

'Naturally.' Mrs Colter gestured to a seat, but Sue stood and looked at her directly.

'We were invited guests, Mrs Colter. My mother had a letter——' She could not pause to choose her words or she would not be able to go on. 'Tell me what happened to Uncle Dryden.'

'He died three months ago, Miss Howard.'

'How did he die?'

'He was thrown off his horse.'

Whatever Sue had expected, it was not a straightforward explanation such as this. 'A fall from a horse?' she echoed.

'Yes. The animal was wild and half-broken.'

'Wasn't he a very good rider?' Sue asked, surprised.

The woman said sharply, 'He was a great rider! It was an accident. The best of horsemen get tossed occasionally.'

'Then why,' Sue persisted, 'is there talk as if his death was not an accident?'

Mrs Colter stood in the centre of the room on her polished floor with her cherished pieces of furniture around her, and her head was stiffly held as though she braced herself. 'I don't know of any talk,' she said steadily.

'Was he riding alone, or was it when the day's work was to begin?'

'He was alone.'

'They weren't working?' questioned Sue.

'No. He decided to ride and went by himself.'

'Rory told me that he was here at the time.'

'Yes, he was.'

Sue was fretted by her lack of co-operation and cried out bitterly, 'Oh, why won't you tell me? He's my uncle, after all!'

'There's nothing to tell, Miss Howard.'

Sue controlled herself with an effort. 'I can see I'm wasting your time and my own.'

She glanced around swiftly, seeing the framed photographs on the mantelpiece, and with no apology for her rudeness walked across to survey them. They were snapshots mainly, and none of any period which might have been before Mrs Colter's time at Undara. Sim as a boy, on a pony. Sim with a sheepdog. There was a photograph cut from a newspaper and framed by a carved surround of native wood. Mrs Colter said softly, 'That was taken at the Picnic Races last year. It's the Boss.'

Sue felt her face flush and a rush of glad emotion. The man's face was weather-seamed and elderly, the eyes deepset and with a daredevil spark. Under the wide felt hat there was a glimpse of white hair and the angular face was amused and wry, as though he had made an ironic comment. There was the self-reliant, competent toughness Sue had seen in other men out here. This was no red-nosed drunkard.

She replaced the photo carefully. 'Thank you for letting me see it,' she said simply. Her feelings must have shown, because the woman spoke in a kinder tone.

'He drank hard and he played hard. Men do, out here.'

'I'm not condemning them, Mrs Colter.'

'He was a good boss. Most men have a story out here. Nobody asks questions.'

Sue watched her. 'He had a story?'

'I guess so. I owed him a lot; he gave Sim a chance. There aren't many who would employ a handicapped boy. This is Sim's home, and this is Sim's life.' At the door, she gestured to the blue sky, the trees and the pale sandy soil. 'Sim loves it here and I'll see that he doesn't lose all he has gained,' she added as Sue walked away.

Sue clenched her hands. I've made matters worse, as usual, she thought. That sounded like a threat.

CHAPTER SEVEN

Sue bypassed the house and opened the gate. Outside the enclosure the brilliance of the sunlight seemed dazzling, and a breeze had sprung up. It whipped grains of sand against her ankles and into her shoes. She went to the saddle shed where Frank Waters sat on a box, heavy legs apart, and a bridle in his thickened fingers. 'Hello, Frank,' she said cheerfully.

He nodded and rumbled something which could have been a greeting or a dismissal. She seated herself on another box and admired the neat stitches mending a torn cheek strap.

'You've had a lot of experience, Frank.'

He nodded again. 'I've been around. Can turn me hand to anything.'

'Could my uncle?'

'Brandy? He was a good bushman, Brandy was. There wasn't much he couldn't do. Cattle, sheep-work, the lot——'

'He loved the bush.' She said it softly, accepting it as truth.

'No cities for him.' The big man put the harness down and gazed past her. 'I went to the city once to work. Terrible tough, it was, too hard and cruel for me. In the city you're a scoundrel straight away if they don't know yer.'

'You've been on Undara for years, Frank?' she asked.

'Off and on. I got me experience up in the north when Brandy first came out from England. Then we went drovin' together—that was before the truck days. Horses, we had.'

Horses. A lifetime of experience with horses, and yet one killed him.

'Then you came here?' she queried.

'No, I went to the Northern Territory for a few years and knocked about there, and Brandy got his bit of dirt.'

She was startled to realise that this was the way he referred to the wide hectares of the large property. 'It's a hard area,' she said.

He agreed cheerfully, his eyes continuing to look beyond her. 'You go from one drought to another out here. It's the smallest rainfall in the country, I'd say. A bit more and it's too much! The country won't stand it. People Inside have no idea what life is like out here.'

'People—Inside?' she probed.

He gestured contemptuously to the far away east. 'People close in to the cities on the coast. We're on the outside, out here.'

Sue, too, stared out at the shimmering landscape where the wind created whirling dust devils in the sand. 'Don't you get lonely, Frank?' she asked soberly.

'I gave me heart once,' he said heavily. 'Never agen. Me an' Brandy had that in common. He said he gave his whole heart once. He tried it once. Never agen.'

She watched him as he took up the bridle again. 'So he came here to forget?'

'Came out to Undara to forget,' he stated definitely.

His hands moved capably on the leather and Sue moistened her lips carefully before she said with forced lightness, 'How did he die, Frank? My Uncle Dryden?'

The deep-set eyes were hooded and the hands still. 'You'd better ask Rory, miss. He can tell you all you need to know.'

She was baffled. She had come up against the bushman's loyalty to a mate, a force she had not realised was so strong. She tried shock tactics. 'You called him Brandy—why?'

143

He grinned with a hint of pride, as at a wilful daring child. 'He never drank anything else.'

'Did he keep a supply here?'

'Mostly.' He was reticent again.

'It's a long way from hotels. What did he do if he ran out?'

'Lately Rory brought it to him. He saw he had what he wanted.'

Ice was on her skin again and she rubbed her arms to restore the warmth as she walked away from the shed. So Rory kept him supplied with drink, did he? She felt her throat grow tight. Rory again . . .

She went back to the shed and fired one last question. 'The car on the track, the burnt-out car. Whose was it?'

Frank stood up and dropped the bridle, and his voice was rough. 'It was your uncle's car. It was burned. Leave things alone here, you and your brother! You're typical city people, blundering in, upsetting things. Get out and leave us alone!'

It was two o'clock, the afternoon had barely begun, and it was a surprise to see the Land Rover at the gate. Penned in the small shed with sand hissing against the walls, Sue had not heard the sound of the motor.

'Where's your brother?' Rory asked impatiently.

'He went for a walk.'

'I want you both to come for a drive,' he commanded.

'Very well. Shall I change?'

'Those clothes will do,' he answered. 'We'll be back by dark.'

They went into the house together, and Kent looked up from the dining table where he had spread out some papers. 'I want to develop some of my stuff, Rory. I'll go back up the track to Yurla and get on with it. That room you

144

blacked out for me will be fine. I've left my equipment there.' Sue was becoming accustomed to the nonchalance with which people set off on long-distance travel in the outback.

Kent glanced towards her. 'Do you want to come, Sue?'

'Nick and I are to go out somewhere with Rory.'

'Shall I come back here tomorrow, Rory?' he asked.

'No,' he said briefly, 'we'll be at Yurla tomorrow. You may as well wait there. I want to talk to Sue and Nick about Dryden's affairs.'

Kent glanced at him quickly. 'I won't be needed,' he said, and flung his papers into a battered briefcase. 'That lot can wait.' He waited until Rory had gone to speak to Clare and then he came closer to Sue. 'I'll put my trip off, Sue, if you need me.'

She said gently, 'Don't do that, Kent. Your work is important and you must be keen to see the results. We'll be at Yurla tomorrow.'

Then her heart sank as she remembered that Nick had made use of Gerry's interest in her. They were to go to Sydney.

He noticed her change of expression. 'What is it, Sue girl?'

She did not resist his embrace but felt no response to his affection, other than friendship. 'We can't stay here, Kent, or go to Yurla. Nick has arranged that we go to Sydney with Gerry.'

He stared at her in dismay and anger. 'Don't be such a fool, Sue! You know what Gerry's interest in you is worth——'

'I can't go to Yurla again,' she repeated.

'Then don't go to Sydney with Gerry! I'll take you.' He put his hands gently beside her cheeks. 'You don't love him, do you?'

'Gerry?'

She was so aghast that he laughed. 'You had me worried for a minute! I thought you'd be too level-headed to fall for his line of talk. Don't accept a ride with him, Sue.'

'We can't stay on, Nick and I,' she protested. 'It's too awkward.'

'Then I'll leave, too, and take you away.'

'No,' she said steadily, 'I won't interrupt your work like that, Kent.'

'I'd do it—for you, Sue.'

She laughed shakily, 'And miss some of the best shots of your career? Shame on you!'

'We'd make a good team,' he suggested brightly.

She was saved from making an answer. Rory was returning, and he glanced keenly from one to the other and his voice sounded harsh.

'Are you ready? Nick has come back.'

'I'll get a warm jacket,' she said.

In her bedroom she lifted the thick padded jacket from a hook behind the door. The quilted garment with a hood had been another of Mrs East's useful suggestions. Sue draped it over her arm and glanced towards the dressing table. She would need nothing else. They were to be back for dinner.

Clare spoke venomously behind her. 'What the devil do you think you're doing?'

Sue had seen her in a rage, but not one as intense as this. Clare's face was white and spots burned red high on her cheekbones.

'We're going for a drive somewhere with Rory.'

Clare came towards Sue as though she would strike her, and bright pinpoints of light blazed in her wide-open, angry eyes.

'*Rory*. So you're going driving with Rory! Do you realise that I'll be alone here?'

'Mrs Colter is here and the men outside. In any case, I see no reason why you shouldn't come——' Sue faltered.

'I see a lot that you'd like hidden, you damnable little schemer! Ever since we came out here you've been trying to take Rory from me.'

'Don't be stupid!' Sue snapped, her poise returning. 'For goodness' sake control yourself, Clare. If you love Rory, you should trust him.'

'You've ruined my whole stay out here,' Clare raged. 'All we've done is run after you and your brother——'

'You won't have to bother with us after today,' Sue promised.

'I'll see to that!' Clare flared. 'You interfere with my life and you'll regret it, Sue Howard!'

When they were leaving Kent drove his battered car to the gate and shouted a farewell above the engine. 'Don't forget!' he called to Sue. 'You must promise to wait for me.'

She felt depressed. She could not see beyond the day and she could give no promise to Kent that she would not go with Gerry. She had a wild desire to get away from everything here, from the hostility of Mrs Colter and Frank. Away from Rory's steely politeness and Clare's jealousy. She didn't like Gerry, but if he would take them to the city they might be wise to accept the ride. They need expect no more from him.

Rory stood, tall and dark, and said dryly, 'If you've finished gazing after Kent——'

'We're ready,' Sue snapped, angered by the uplifted eyebrow and the expression on his face. What was the matter with him *now*?

He gestured to the utility parked nearby and Clare came out of the gate as they seated themselves. Her face was set and she flashed a glance towards Sue, and there was waspish anger in the look. 'You seem determined that I must be left out,' she said to Rory.

Though it was a complaint her voice was one of submissive charm and he replied gently.

'I've explained to you—this is Sue and Nick's affair. We'll be back before evening.'

There were tight lines beside Clare's lips as she battled to control herself, and her steely will triumphed.

He leaned out as he started the motor. 'Mrs Colter has gone out on the run with Sim, but will be back soon. Tell them we've gone to Red Tors. Somebody must be told the direction we've taken in case of accidents. Tell her Red Tors, Clare.'

She nodded briefly and stood back. He's so undemonstrative, Sue thought, pitying her a little, he gives her few outward signs of his love. It must be hard for her . . .

The vehicle gathered speed and they passed the sheds. Frank had gone from the harness room and the door was closed. The track curved beyond the woolshed, and dust swirled up to hide the buildings. 'Where are we going?' Nick demanded.

'I want you to see more of your uncle's property before I talk to you,' Rory stated.

The wind died away as they drove across a plain where red and purple pebbles covered the surface. Then it became broken, cut by short, sharp gullies where the utility tilted down inclines and reared up steep banks to the other side. There were puffs of grey cloud to the north, folded and rounded, which joined into cottonwool whiteness and boiled up into the purity of the sky. A falcon floated above them, but there was no other sign of life.

'It's dry country,' Nick observed.

'Desert fringe,' Rory said briefly, 'temperatures can be high out here.'

'It's damned dreary,' Nick said disparagingly.

'It depends on your outlook,' the older man replied, and concentrated on the track.

Water glittered ahead, but it was a mirage, for the lake was bone-white and dry when they drew near. After an interval they saw a bore, and Rory gestured towards it.

'Dryden planned bores at reasonable distances so that he could move his flock from place to place and guard against over-grazing. This one is saline and not fit for human consumption, but sheep and kangaroos can tolerate it.'

Nick was defensive when he was with Rory, almost as though he were afraid of him, Sue thought. He sounded young and unsure of himself when he reverted to sarcasm, instead of sophisticated, as he hoped.

'Over-grazing? On what?'

'You'll see,' returned Rory.

Sue tried to be more conversational. 'Wasn't it supposed to be an inland sea aeons ago?'

He nodded agreement. 'Do you find it hard to picture it? Later the land rose and became an area of rivers, forests and life, and, in time, the great diprotodons, giant wombats and huge kangaroos lived here.'

'I have read that skeletons are found——'

'Yes,' he agreed, 'trapped in the lakes in the ooze as the moisture dried out and another era of change occurred. Many of us have fossilised bones and petrified wood around the homesteads.'

A cover of saltbush appeared and Sue saw a sheet of yellow ahead. They were wildflowers which stretched to the horizon, the colours, clearer in contrast with the red of the earth and the blue sky, than she had seen anywhere. Acacias were blooming and low wattles were decked with yellow.

'You see the change?' Rory asked them both. 'There's been good rain over several hundred kilometres of this area.

149

It happens like that. It can be bountiful in one part and drought beside it.'

There was another lake bed, reedy and waterless, but green shoots stood among yellowed tussocks. The creamy sand was touched with verdant life and kangaroos and emus were dotted across the expanse.

Sue thought it was one of the happiest periods she had known since they had arrived—to travel with Rory in the intimacy of the utility's cabin, to hear him speak of the land he loved and be able to share with him, briefly, the interest of the surroundings. Clare had been wiser than she knew to be jealous of me, Sue confessed to herself. I love Rory, but nobody will know it ... ever.

They followed the rim of the old lake bed where yellow and purple flowers were spread in profusion. Rory nodded to low, mauve hills which crouched ahead like ancient monsters which had roamed there when the world was new. In the brilliant sunlight Sue saw the lavender colouring change to red as they drew closer, nor were the crags rounded as they had appeared when softened by distance. There were deep shadows cast by fangs of rock and light touched surfaces which glowed orange and terracotta.

When they reached the tors she saw that there were beefwoods and gums on the flat land around, but Rory drove past their meagre shade to place the vehicle close to a stony cliff where a shadow lay black on the sand below.

Sue stepped out among hardy paper daisies and the purple of pea. A group of kangaroos hopped away from the shelter of thorny trees, unhurried, and paused to survey them.

Nick smiled and his youthful enthusiasm wiped out his dislike of Rory temporarily. 'It's good to see them so quiet.'

'Your uncle wouldn't allow shooters on the place,' answered Rory. 'The only track in from outside has to pass the

Outstation so he could keep an eye on poachers.'

They followed him into a widening cleft between two of the eroded mountain peaks. The tors were more extensive than they had appeared in the deceptive flatness of the country with its lack of perspective. They walked for some time and it grew very hot in the enclosed place, and Sue wished they had not carried their jackets with them, as it seemed an unnecessary burden.

The cleft gradually widened, became a valley of stone smoothed by water in days when streams had run over it. The woolly mass of cloud thickened and rolled closer, dimming the sun, and red drained from the rock to leave it grey and forbidding.

Then it cooled and the temperature dropped noticeably. At last they came to another break in a rock wall which shut off the end of the valley. It was a dark cleft, a crevice, and a grey, weathered tree trunk had fallen over the gap.

Sue and Nick stopped. It was the end of the walk, for there was no place to go. They could see nothing of interest, or any reason for Rory to bring them so far into the lonely place. He stood and watched them for a moment and it was clear that he was agitated and indecisive. Sue thought that he hesitated briefly before he spoke again.

'This is the end of your search,' he said in a strange and quiet voice. 'You've reached the end.'

'Give me a hand, Nick,' Rory said at last.

He went forward and began to lift the log. Puzzled, Nick helped him to swing it aside from where it masked the opening. The cleft looked no larger, but Rory gestured to Sue to move into it.

There was a sharp angle hidden by shadow and she turned the corner, hearing the others follow closely.

The cleft opened dramatically to a small gorge, cliffverandahed and hidden. Sue paused, and Rory touched her shoulder. 'Go forward—under the cliff.'

On the walls of the cave-like area were aboriginal drawings. A snake in red and yellow ochre, boomerangs and stone axes. Hands had been outlined by holding them on the rock and the ochre blown round them by the mouth. The protected place had preserved the colours and outlines in wonderful clarity.

There were other markings on slabs of rock and the two young ones studied them closely. The valley was a treasure-house of ancient art.

'What are they?' Sue asked.

'Petroglyphs,' Rory said. 'They're incised by painful effort with stone tools.'

'Figures of men, and animals,' Nick pointed out.

'Millions of years old,' Sue murmured, awed.

'They're pecked out of the rock by using two stones,' Rory stated, 'one was used as a chisel and one as a hammer.'

Under the shelter the carvings were clear and deep, but time and the elements had dulled those on the flat surfaces where sun and rain could work on them. They walked about for some time, observing and exclaiming. In the distance they heard a rumble of thunder, but were too engrossed to notice.

Nick turned to Rory, 'What's the story?'

'This is part of it. Sit down and let's talk.'

The clouds had thickened and it grew gloomy while they waited for him to speak. Sue saw him glance quickly at the sky, but there seemed to be little rain in the thunderheads.

'Over the border,' he began, 'much of the corner country has been acquired by the National Parks for Ecology when graziers went down in the wool slump. Others are to be bought as they become available, and the area kept for regeneration of wildlife and for study——'

Nick frowned. 'What has this to do with us?'

'Your uncle, too, grew concerned for the country as he grew older; he saw the effect the introduced sheep and cattle have had on the life which had existed here for centuries before the white man came. The removal of plant cover denied shelter to small marsupials and bird life.'

'What about his sheep?' Sue asked.

'He began to decrease his flock so that he could regenerate some of his land, because the balance is so delicate in this desert fringe country with the low rainfall. You get these narrow strips of rain at times which bring vegetation across the land, and the wildlife follows.' Rory seemed to speak to Sue rather than Nick, and she watched his face as he explained her uncle's dream. 'He felt that these animals and birds, unique in the world, must have areas where they can survive.'

Nick tried to keep the toughness in his voice. 'I can't see how you come into it.'

'I've been in it for some time. Your uncle was my friend, as well as a neighbour. He had an accident at the beginning of the year. He was coming home from town and ran into a tree with his car. Petrol spilled and the vehicle became engulfed in flames.'

Nick eased the sling which supported his arm, and Sue saw that his eyes were alert and suspicious as he watched Rory.

'The car on the track?' she put in.

'Yes. He was badly burned and spent weeks in hospital. He had skin grafts and all the rest of it——' He looked directly at Sue again. 'He suffered a great deal.'

'He didn't die from his burns,' Nick stated.

'He insisted on returning home, though his treatment was not complete. He sent Sim to Yurla to fetch me and I came

153

to him at once. From that day we were the only people to see him.'

Bitter memory tinged Rory's voice. 'He was unrecognisable. His face was badly scarred and he insisted that he would see nobody from outside. In the past, when he needed company, he would go to town and drink with his friends. Now he ordered liquor brought with his supplies or, if he ran out, I would bring it.'

'You kept him supplied?' Nick sneered. 'You saw to that, didn't you? So that you could work on him and influence him into making a will which benefited you.'

'He willed Undara to me,' Rory said grimly.

'So it's yours.' Nick swung away as though he couldn't bear the truth now that he knew it. 'You damned well took it over!'

'This is the reason.' Rory waved a hand to the native relics. 'He regarded these as too precious to allow indiscriminate and careless handling of them, or to have them ruined by vandals. Many of the fine aboriginal drawings in caves in the north have been defaced and destroyed, initials scrawled over them! They've been ruined and lost for ever.'

'What do you expect to do?' Nick turned again, and his eyes were hard.

'This is the crux of the story. Dryden found this place, and he made me swear that proper arrangements would be made to guard it. This will take time. The area is to be a sanctuary for wildlife and a proper authority set up to provide a ranger to care for the native relics.' He said forcibly, 'We promised secrecy, Mrs Colter and Sim, Frank and myself. I am responsible——'

'So we caused trouble when we arrived,' Sue said simply.

'Yes. Nick's threats of legal action—can't you see that publicity at this stage would ruin everything?'

154

'You wouldn't want that!' Nick said bitterly.

'Dryden knew men,' returned Rory. 'He knew that if this valley is exposed to publicity before safeguards are set up it will be despoiled. There'll be people in here with four-wheeled drive vehicles. They'll chip layers of rock away and carry them off as souvenirs, breaking and ruining others in senseless destroying!'

'Surely they wouldn't!' Sue cried.

'They do. It has happened in other areas.' Rory said firmly, 'I gave Dryden my word that all that could be done to protect these rare art forms—will be done.'

'Preserved for posterity,' Sue murmured.

Rory looked at her, and it was as though a flash of understanding passed between them. 'You see what he hoped for?' he said.

'It leaves us out on a limb, doesn't it?' Nick protested.

'If your uncle's wishes for Undara are carried out, you will be, as you say, on a limb,' Rory agreed.

'If we insist on a share then this must be lost?' asked Sue.

Rory said patiently, 'Not this alone, the whole concept! If the sanctuary is to be of benefit, the sheep must be kept out of this end of the property. It cuts the carrying capacity in half. Only someone like myself, who has land, can run it. There will be enough to cover expenses, no more.'

A loud rumble of thunder over the caps of the tors brought the two Londoners to a startled awareness of the storm. The big clouds were bluish-purple and they saw lightning fork down from the rolling mass.

Sue jumped to her feet. She had no wish to be imprisoned in the confined space with lightning playing on the heights above her. 'Oh, let's go!' she cried.

Rory muttered something about 'a dry storm', but she did not listen. The men followed her to the concealed entrance, and once they were through the narrow aperture Rory slid the tree trunk into place.

Big drops of rain began to patter down, marking the rock surfaces with coin-sized spots of wetness. Sue slipped on the smoothness of wet rock and wished she had worn rubber soled shoes.

There was a cannon-like sound, reverberating in the valley, and lightning struck on the heights above, followed by another shattering clap of thunder. Sue screamed and lost her footing. As she fell to her hands and knees Rory bent and lifted her. She stood, shaking, her head pressed to his shoulder, and he held her close soothing her as though she had been a child.

She became conscious of his embrace and muttered something about her shoes.

'I didn't warn you that we'd be on rock,' he said briefly. He kept his hand under her elbow as they walked forward and she longed to be able to clasp his hand with natural ease. Nick had raced ahead to stand at the valley mouth. Rory paused, astonished, and Sue baulked as she saw the threshing, bending scrub and tumbleweed bowling before the wind.

'Isn't it wild?' she gasped.

'We were sheltered,' Rory explained. 'There isn't much rain in it, I'm afraid.'

Lightning seared the air, finding the shortest route to the earth. The skeletons of the old mountains echoed the thunder which followed each enormous electrical discharge. The wild wind blew raindrops into their faces, and a weird light lit the hills to a macabre purple.

'Wait here,' Rory ordered. 'It's a bit out of the blow. I'll bring the utility to you.'

He ran past the tumbled rocks close to the cliff side. They saw him place a hand on the door of the utility as another vivid streak of lightning struck a twisted white gum which struggled for survival in a fissure on the heights. The two watchers saw the claw-like branches disintegrate and the faulted face of rock, which had provided the crack for the questing roots, bulged and fell away.

The heavy stone face appeared to break into many pieces as it tumbled forward and outwards. Sue screamed loudly, uselessly, and began to run. She thought she heard Nick shout and knew that he, too, ran with her. There was another sharp crack of thunder and the wind stilled as suddenly as it had sprung up, and the rain drew away across the lake in a veil of white.

Sue was on her knees, anguished, tearing at the jagged rocks with her bare hands. Rory's filthy, bloodstained face was all she could see. Nick stood staring, until she screamed at him and he came to his knees beside her.

'He's been hit by the edge, that's all——' He was trying to reassure himself as well as his sister.

They dragged the big man free and Sue brushed the dark hair back from the dust-marked forehead. She did not realise that he was looking at her in a dazed fashion.

'The ute——?' he whispered.

She turned and surveyed it. She shuddered, 'Thank God you hadn't got into it!'

'As bad as that?' She saw his teeth clench. 'Are you—both——?'

'We're all right,' Nick said urgently.

'I've got a few bruises, I think.' He shut his mouth tight on the words as though willing his injuries to be slight. 'Help me up, Nick.'

Sue saw that the effort was painful to him, but he stood at last, growing paler as they watched. His face was grim when he saw the remains of the utility truck.

'You're right. I'm lucky I wasn't sitting there.'

'What do we do now?' Nick sounded stunned and at a loss.

'Wait, I'm afraid. Clare knows where we are. When we're not back for dinner Mrs Colter will send someone out for us.' Rory drew a deep breath and attempted to stand alone, but Sue felt his weight return heavily to their supporting arms. 'Over there.' He nodded towards a slab of rock and when they reached it, he sank to it quickly.

Sue saw the effort he made to stay upright. 'You're hurt. You may as well admit it.'

'Some ribs, I think,' he said thickly, and winced as he moved his arms. 'And—my leg——' Greyness tinged the pallor and he leaned down so that his head was between his knees.

Sue was about to ask if he would like a drink of water and remembered there was none. Whatever had been in the utility was buried beneath the rock fall.

Rory said, between gritted teeth, 'They'll be out soon——' He slid to the sand at their feet.

The clouds broke and sharp shadows were cast by the setting sun on the angles of rock.

'Get his matches, Nick,' Sue ordered, and he fumbled in the man's pocket and slid them out. 'Come on! A fire,' she urged. 'It's getting cold.'

It was occupation for her brother and she was glad to see more colour return to Rory's face as the twigs crackled and the wood began to blaze. The sand had absorbed the brief shower and was drying out. He straightened his body slowly where he lay and muttered weakly, 'This is a fine turn-out!'

'They'll come soon,' Sue encouraged him. 'The fire will keep us warm.'

Between them they eased up the trouser leg and inspected Rory's knee. It was discolouring quickly, and she bound it firmly with her scarf, then they helped him take off his shirt. From the shirt she improvised a wide bandage to strap his rips and eased the heavy jacket over his shoulders and arms. As she buttoned it he said, 'I haven't had anyone button me into anything since I was a child.'

She pretended to be brisk. 'You're having it now—and no arguments!' She had to admire his control and the manner in which he relegated his pain to a secondary place. She and Nick sat near the fire too, and watched the sunset paint the sky in gaudy colours and the clouds disperse and evaporate as though the storm had never been. Rory's eyes were closed.

'Mrs Colter knows all about things, doesn't she?' Nick began to get anxious as time passed.

'She'll send Sim in the Land Rover,' Sue assured him confidently.

'Clare will be worried,' Nick added.

They had to wait, there was no choice. The chill of night increased. Rory was conscious again but seemed dazed and uncaring of his surroundings; Nick went off and foraged for more wood for the fire and Sue helped him with larger pieces because he was handicapped with his arm in the sling.

As they pulled the heavy butt of a log towards the fire he whispered, 'I'm thirsty.'

'We all are,' she responded. 'Let's hope they won't be long now. Rory needs care and they'll have to call on the Flying Doctor.'

'If I set out to walk——' He baulked at his own suggestion. 'I doubt if I could find the way.'

'There's no need. We wait.'

They watched the darkness deepen and, later, the moon rose, bronzed and magnificent, to lift to the heavens in white purity, but there were no headlights on the track. The

159

fire burned low and was replenished again.

'You may as well sleep for a while.' Rory spoke suddenly in a dry half-voice which conveyed that he was avoiding deep breaths.

'I'm not tired,' Nick said sharply, as though he had been accused of weakness.

An hour passed and Sue saw that her brother was sleeping, curled uncomfortably as near the fire as he could bear. Frozen on his back and roasted on his front, she thought gloomily, as I am. But Rory isn't complaining...

She could hear his breathing, uneven and ragged, and knew that he was chilled. She gathered the cold hands in hers and let her warmth bring life to them again. The strong hands lay flaccid and unresisting as she massaged them and she felt the skin grow warmer and suppleness return to the fingers. She pulled the sleeves of his jacket down to cover them.

Her movements roused Nick and he lurched to his feet. His eyes were bleared with sleep. 'Haven't they come yet?' he demanded.

She said patiently, 'They may have decided to wait until daylight.'

'Why the hell would they do that? They have headlights! In any case, you could drive across country by the moonlight tonight.'

'They'll come,' she soothed. 'Kent has gone to Yurla, you remember?'

'That leaves the Colters, Frank—and Clare.'

'Clare isn't experienced, and Mrs Colter would know that we'd come to no harm for the night. She's a bushwoman.'

'I wish to heaven they'd hurry up. I'm cold,' Nick said, but there was little of the old complaint in his voice. He crouched on his heels by the fire, in the stockman's style and after a few minutes he said, 'We can still upset the arrangements here. We are Uncle Dryden's heirs.'

Sue said quietly, 'Yes, I know.' Her uncle's dream for the semi-desert country, of saving it for future generations, had caught her imagination and she was jarred to find that Nick had not caught the grandeur of the scheme. He was thinking of the profit which might be his.

When morning came Sue felt Rory's skin and was alarmed to feel the heat of it. She narrowed her eyes and peered hopefully to the distance where golden bars of sunlight lay across the land.

The night had been a hard time of waiting, but the morning hours dragged unbearably. Nick climbed to a high vantage point at the top of a tor. While he was away Rory heaved a sigh and winced as he tried to move. A stubble of beard darkened his face and his eyes were worried.

'What in God's name are they doing?'

Sue tried to comfort him, but he did not listen. He tried to turn his arm so that he could see his wristwatch, and she saw shock on his face when he saw the time.

'You'll have to leave me,' he said firmly.

'Leave you?' She was aghast. 'What are we to do?'

'Walk! Something has gone wrong, you realise that? They wouldn't be so long coming——' his voice faded.

'Perhaps Clare misunderstood?' But she remembered how clearly he had explained their destination to Clare. She could not have made a mistake when telling Mrs Colter where they had gone, could she?

Nick came down a steep slope with stones rattling under his feet and his haggard face was set in weary lines. 'There's not a sign. No dust, nothing.' He glared at Rory as though he had been to blame.

Purpose was clear on the older man's face. 'Give me a hand,' he commanded fiercely.

Again they propped and aided and he struggled to his feet, but Nick, reluctant as he was to admit it, had to agree that it would not be possible for him to move more than a few painful yards. Rory sank to a rock, defeated, and there was a pause.

'Get into the shade with him, Sue,' Nick said suddenly, 'it's getting hot. I'm walking.'

Automatic protest came to her lips. 'Oh, Nick, you can't!'

Rory looked at the young man directly. 'It's up to you.'

'Give me directions,' Nick was curt, 'that's all I ask.'

As she listened and tried to memorise too, Sue wondered if her brother would be able to cope with what lay ahead. The desert burrs spiking his feet through the heavy rubber of his shoe-soles, the sun which would fry his skin... Would the halting directions stay in his mind then? Would he begin to wander and lose the identity of east and west and roam, lost, into the waterless loneliness?

Nick stood and looked at Rory. 'I'll go, damn you!'

'It's our only hope.' Rory's voice dragged. 'Something has gone wrong.'

Nick said contemptuously, 'Perhaps it has. Perhaps this is another of your tricks! We'll see, won't we?'

CHAPTER EIGHT

Nick dragged his hat over his eyes, hitched his sling to a more comfortable position, and walked away from them. His figure was clear for a long time and grew smaller until Sue could no longer pick out the tiny moving object as he disappeared over the horizon.

With Nick gone the hours drew out again. Sue lay on the sand and let the warmth of the sun seep into her body. She slept and woke to see Rory looking at her.

'What time is it?' she asked.

He glanced at the sun. 'About eleven.'

'How long will it take him to walk, Rory?'

'I would know if I were the one to go,' he returned grimly.

'You mean that Nick is weaker?'

'He's new to the conditions.'

'It's lucky it's not summer,' she said, frowning. She saw him try to ease his leg into another position and jumped to her feet. 'Let me help.'

'You've done enough,' he said wearily. 'I should be helping you.'

The strained lines of his mouth under the stubble of beard moved her to an inexplicable pity. 'It's getting hot here,' she said, 'the sun has moved round. Do you think you could move to the shade again?'

His smile was bitter and deprecating. 'I can crawl.' He jerked his body forward over the sand and sank back with a slab of rock to support him.

Sue could see the dryness of his compressed lips and knew that her own were desiccated too. Talking was becoming a labour and she was obsessed with thoughts of long, chilled glasses of water, beaded with dew and with droplets of moisture running on the sides.

Rory gestured. 'Sit closer—I can't talk very loudly.'

She moved to his side and he turned his head to look at her. He looked paler and she regretted that there was so little she could do for him.

She heard him whisper, 'I'm sorry, Sue.'

She stretched her lips in a painful smile. 'Don't worry about me.'

Almost absently his hand closed over hers, gritty, dry and hot. 'You've had so much to face since you came out here.'

'It just happened that way,' she defended.

'Are you sure? You don't think that I tried to kill you? Or frighten you away?'

'No. Not you, Rory.' Afterwards she was glad she had given him the assurance of her trust. She did not regret it, later . . .

He was silent again and his head fell towards her and his body slumped as he dozed. She put her arms about him and supported him, and his hair was rough, spiky and dusty against her cheek. Sue sat, rigid, watching the horizon, and waited for the vehicles from Undara.

There was nobody to witness the gentleness of her clasp or the love on her face. It was a brief interval when she could be alone with him and give him her strength and help. It would be something to remember . . . it would be all she would have.

It was late afternoon before the vehicles arrived and she propped Rory against the rock and walked out into the sun to meet them. Frank and Sim jumped out of the Land Rover and Frank's rough-cast face was concerned as he looked down at Rory.

Kent drove up behind them and came to Sue. 'You must have thought we weren't coming.' He held her close briefly. 'Poor old girl!'

Sim and Frank had lifted a light frame from the vehicle and the three men lifted Rory on to it. It took some manipulation to get it into the back of the Land Rover, but they were ready and were driving away before Sue realised it.

Kent led her to his car and gave her the water bottle. 'Not too much now—a little at a time. You're to go to bed at Undara. The Flying Doctor will pick Rory up at the strip as soon as he arrives there.'

'I'm quite well,' she protested.

'You look worn out. Mrs Colter has a bed ready for you. We tucked Nick up, the lad did a heroic walk. He was dead beat and his feet badly blistered.'

'Why didn't Mrs Colter send help earlier?' she asked.

'She got her lines crossed, evidently, and thought that Rory had gone to the Red Sandhills area, so we spent our time looking out there! A wasted night. I came back from Yurla in the early night hours when I heard you weren't back, but didn't bring men from there as we thought there was no urgency at that stage.'

'Our tracks,' she protested feebly.

'Obliterated by the storm.' He smiled at her. 'Go on, snuggle down and sleep.'

Kent took her directly to the house, but she could not rest until she was told that the plane had taxied away from the airstrip, carrying Rory to hospital. She did not see Clare; it was Clare's place to be at Rory's side.

With a heavy heart she lay on the bed and Kent tiptoed in and eased the shoes from her aching feet.

'I'm filthy,' she mumbled.

'Who cares? You had the meal Mrs Colter prepared for you? Go to sleep now.'

She closed her eyes against tears which threatened to swamp her. It was over. For a brief time Rory had been dependent on her; she had been the one to comfort him and share his moments of anxiety and pain.

It was over. He had gone—with Clare.

She let the dark despair and weariness swamp her and did not hear Kent close the door, or Mrs Colter's voice in answer to him.

'Did Mr Darker come yesterday, Mrs Colter?' Sue asked.

'He certainly did.'

Her face was set and forbidding and Sue wondered what reason she had to dislike the young man. He had not been a welcome caller, as far as the housekeeper was concerned. He had called for Sue and Nick and they had not been there. Another avenue closed . . .

Sue stood at the door of the kitchen, baffled by the woman's manner. She accepted the hostility. 'I know you don't like us, Mrs Colter, and I'm sorry that my brother and I have to stay at Undara. I'll see that we cause as little trouble as possible.'

Mrs Colter seemed taken aback by the direct attack. 'I'm not the boss here, Miss Howard.'

'Neither am I,' Sue said simply. 'Nor likely to be.' She kept her hand away from the wall as Mrs Colter left her, though she felt she needed the support. In the bathroom she bathed sketchily, feeling weak and dizzy. What a time to get a cold! She could feel the heaviness of head, the prickling at the back of her throat that heralded a bad bout. She pulled a nightgown over her shoulders and put on her gown, then she went to the bedroom which Nick occupied and he grinned at her briefly.

'You look a wreck,' he told her.

'I'll recover. We can't leave today, though, I don't feel well enough.'

'I'm not moving,' he said with a grimace.

'We'll go as soon as we can,' she said firmly.

'Don't sound so bossy, Sue!'

'Just see you don't give Mrs Colter any extra work,' she snapped.

Nick's eyes widened in surprise. 'What's biting you? I'm the one who walked all that distance—I've got blisters to prove it.'

'I know,' she said, more gently.

'Gerry's gone too,' he moaned.

'We couldn't have gone with him, Nick. I've had enough of leaning on others to sort out our future. We'll do our own thinking from now on.' She went away and left him staring after her. She sat on her bed and gradually eased herself into it. A cold! Of all the stupid handicaps! Now, of all times.

Kent did not come in until lunch time and she did not ask where he had been; she didn't care. His face grew concerned as he looked at her. 'Why, Sue! I thought you'd be fit to go——'

'Go where?' She shivered and burned at the same time.

'To Yurla. Rory left a message that I was to take you and Nick to the homestead until he returns from hospital.'

More dictatorial decisions! She waited for the sustaining flare of anger, but none came. 'We won't be going there, Kent,' she said.

He pushed the hair back from her hot forehead. 'You won't be going anywhere, girlie, I can see that.'

'What news?' she asked anxiously.

'Rory has been patched up, but he's chafing at the bit in hospital, it seems. I don't envy the nurses!'

'How is Nick now?' She switched topics quickly.

'Alternating between bed and a verandah chair. He's picking up. You can't keep youth down.'

After lunch Kent returned and sat on the side of the bed, and Sue heard his voice as he chatted on about the day and his activities. She had difficulty keeping track of it. She heard him mention Clare and opened her eyes muzzily.

'She went on the plane, too!'

He nodded. 'Trust our Clare! Always on the ball. She doesn't miss a trick, that one.'

'She loves Rory,' Sue stated.

'You mean Rory's money and comfortable position and being Mrs Stevens of Yurla!' Kent gave a hoot of derision.

Her voice was shocked. 'Oh, Kent, no!'

He nodded. 'Dadda has married again and that means another woman has first go at his wallet. Clare has been left flat as far as handouts are concerned. Didn't you realise?'

She tried to think coherently, but a dismayed anguish gripped her. So Rory was being cheated! Clare did not love him. What hope was there for a marriage based on such treachery?

It was none of her business, she must remember that! She was an outsider and whatever Clare and Rory would do was not her concern. It drove sleep from her, however, and after Kent left she stared at the wall where light flickered and danced through trees at the window. Clare would be sitting beside Rory's bed now, leaning over in her pose of gentle compassion, and here, at Undara, the two Howards were loitering, a problem and a burden.

Get well. Get well quickly, Sue ordered herself.

The next day Kent drove to Yurla again to work in the darkroom, and Nick went with him. Sue was alone in the house when Mrs Colter brought her cup of tea at eleven o'clock. 'I'll get in touch with the Flying Doctor for you, Miss Howard, if you want it.'

'There's no need,' Sue said. 'I'm feeling better. You've been very kind, Mrs Colter.'

The woman stood straight and tall and her voice was low. 'Do you think so?'

Sue's eyes were tired. 'You would know my uncle better than most people, Mrs Colter.'

She thought the remark would earn her a crushing reproof or icy silence but the controlled face softened. 'I did.'

'I wish I'd known him,' Sue murmured.

'He was a wild man, Miss Howard, but a man you could trust. I owed him a lot.'

Sue nodded. You loved him ... She knew she would never say it, but the words hung unacknowledged between them. She heard the crisp steps going away through the house, footsteps which indicated impatience of weakness and indecision. Mrs Colter had learned in a hard school, and life had honed away the softness in her.

Kent came back in the evening and he and Nick swept into the house with overflowing energy and high spirits.

'I've finished some of the work,' he said. 'I have things to show you!'

'The photos?' Sue asked. She had bathed and dressed in the slack suit which she had with her and felt a little better.

'After dinner,' he promised. He went to the kitchen and she heard him talking to Mrs Colter and getting an indulgent laugh in response. After the meal was over Mrs Colter, Sim and Frank joined them in the big dining room.

Again Sue saw in Kent the nervousness of an artist before a performance. He became different suddenly.

'Some are complete failures,' he told them. 'Some are passable,' he put a thick folder on the table in front of Sue and she slid the photos out carefully. 'They'll be enlarged to a size suitable for exhibition,' he explained.

Some of the pictures were in colour and others were striking in black and white. It was a record of their stay in Australia, Sue thought, torn by nostalgic remembrances as the scenes appeared one by one. The moods, the colour of the land, a curve of horizon offset by a stark dead tree. The drama of a fantastic sunset with the extraordinary brilliance of light seen at no other time.

Her fingers faltered when she lifted the photograph which he had taken on the first morning of the trip, the first time she had posed for him. Her skin appeared luminous and sun touched her fair, rippling hair which made a delicate contrast to the rough bark of the enormous tree. The soft morning light gave the picture a distinct ethereal beauty and she heard Nick grunt in satisfaction and saw Sim's quick fingers as he conveyed a message.

Kent nodded, pleased. 'I agree, Sim.'

I wish I had learned to communicate with Sim, Sue thought, and smiled up at him. It's too late now . . .

'He says it's very beautiful,' Mrs Colter said dryly.

Sue flushed. 'It's flattering. You are talented, Kent.'

'This one is a flop,' he admitted bitterly. The horses galloping across the paddock, the day they arrived.

'You can give it to me,' she said flippantly, 'for a memento. I think it's very good.'

'The corners are blurred,' he pointed out, disappointed.

'You're a perfectionist,' Nick jibed, 'it looks great to me.'

'Have it, Sue, if you like,' Kent offered. 'It's not good enough to show.'

She laughed. 'Thank you. Your offer doesn't sound very gracious, but I know what you mean.' She put it aside; there was a crisply outlined study of a man on a galloping horse and she recognised Rory and the black stallion. It was clear that the horse was spirited but that the man was the master.

'The Boss's horse,' Mrs Colter said quietly.

Dryden Brooks . . . Sue studied it more carefully before passing the print along. There had been an undertone in the woman's voice and Frank's beefy hands had become rigid as he took the picture. Sim moved uneasily and pushed the photo aside after a brief scrutiny.

That is the horse that killed my uncle, Sue thought painfully. They could not have spelled it out more clearly, any of them.

The backlighting of wool on a sheep's back caught her

attention and she tried to take an intelligent interest as the photos came up, one by one, for their perusal. The open plains of Undara. Sandhills ... the lonely wreck of the old house ... cattle ... horsemen ... the mustering camp ...

After they had been through them all Nick pointed to one. 'That's the pick of them.'

'The signpost?' Kent lifted it and stared at it critically. 'You do look little and lost, Sue.'

It gave her a pang of self-consciousness to see how clearly his probing lens had caught her expression of sadness and loneliness. It was like being stripped before them and she hurriedly slipped the study between others out of sight.

'I wouldn't mind seeing your exhibition, Kent,' enthused Nick.

Mrs Colter stood and thanked Kent briefly, and Sim flicked a quick message on nimble fingers which made Kent laugh. Frank got to his feet heavily.

'Would you go to London to see them, Frank?' Nick probed.

'I wouldn't go to any city to see anything,' he said curtly.

Sue touched the photos with her fingertips. 'The best of luck with them, Kent. You've produced some outstanding work there.'

'You can see why I wanted to get out to Yurla,' he enthused.

'There are none of Clare,' Nick said suddenly, 'she was in several. How come?'

Kent's face wore a strange expression. 'They weren't a success.' He turned away as though he wanted to say no more, and Sue picked the folder up and replaced the pictures carefully.

'Guard these with your life, Kent.'

'It might mean a new life,' he agreed. 'London—here I

come!' There was elation as well as trepidation in his face.

'You know they're good,' Sue said as they went into the living room for the evening, 'why not admit it?'

'There are thousands who are "good", Sue,' he said earnestly. 'I need to be a bit better and have a lot of luck. Few make it to the top, you know.'

She said quietly, 'You'll make it, Kent. I know it.'

He was about to speak, to put a hand out to her when Nick came in.

'Haven't you lit the fire? It's getting cold. Let's settle down and be comfortable.'

'We must find out about a plane, Kent.' Sue stood so that she could be more confident. 'Nick and I must go.'

'Go to Brisbane to Aunt Essie. I'll see she keeps tabs on you until I can get back.'

'It would be an imposition,' Sue protested.

'She'll love having you,' Kent declared, leaning back in a big chair.

'We'll see,' she said quietly.

'I wonder when Rory will be back?' Nick asked.

'A few days yet,' Kent asserted. 'I'm going up the track tomorrow, so you can pick up your things from Yurla and catch a plane from there.'

Rory wouldn't be there. I couldn't bear to see him again, Sue thought. It should be a brief visit to Yurla and we'll go . . .

The next morning Kent took Sue's bag out to the car and Nick slouched in to lean on the dressing table.

'I'm damned sorry to go, Sue. I can see why Uncle Dryden liked it here. It gets you.'

'I feel it, too,' she admitted, and gathered up her parka.

'Are we letting Rory win the battle for Undara?'

'What's he getting out of it except responsibility, Nick?

172

You can fight the will, if you must. I won't have any part in it.'

'I rather like the thought of it,' he admitted. 'A good memorial to the old boy, Sue, eh? Tramping in from the Red Tors I had time to look at the place and I can see what he meant. The balance is delicate——' Dreams touched his eyes for a moment. 'Oh, well! It's down to earth for us, Sue, and back to the city grind!'

He went to the car and Sue stood, memorising the view of the garden from the bedroom window and the distant smudge, a mauve mound on the horizon, which was Red Tors.

'Can I have a word with you, Miss Howard?'

She turned, smiling. 'Yes, Mrs Colter. I was coming to say goodbye. Will you give messages to Frank and Sim for me, please?'

She nodded. Without preamble she said, 'I pulled the branch down at the camp—with my whip.'

Sue nodded. 'I wondered why you carried it at night.'

'I'd moved the bedrolls earlier. Nobody noticed. They're used to me being about and I could pretend that it was a job I had to do. I waited until you were out of bed and I flicked the whip over the branch and gave a good tug.'

'Why?' Sue asked quietly.

'We—I hoped that you'd be scared away. You were fresh out and new to bush life—you looked soft and delicate——'

'We? Was there someone else who wanted us to go?'

'I speak for myself. I thought you might go away, that you'd think the conditions were raw and hard.'

'I like it, but—we're going, Mrs Colter. We won't fight for Undara. We like Uncle Dryden's idea for the future of the place.'

'You're going?' Mrs Colter asked.

173

'Yes. We'll go, but not because of the things that happened to us.'

'I don't know of any other episodes, Miss Howard.'

'The cattle?' probed Sue.

The woman shrugged. 'Cattle are tricky. It was just one of those things.'

'Who was in charge of the cattle at that hour? Whose shift was it?'

'I wouldn't know.' Mrs Colter turned to leave.

'I can find out,' Sue said musingly. 'I can ask at Yurla.'

The woman faced her again. 'What's the point?'

'None, now—but I'd like to know who hated us enough to want to kill us.'

'You weren't meant——' Mrs Colter bit the words back.

'We weren't meant to be killed? Perhaps the stockman didn't know that my brother's over-developed sense of drama had led us to sleep outside the circle of stones.' Sue's voice was hard.

Mrs Colter's thin face set. 'It was a fool thing—dangerous.'

'Frank? Or Sim?'

She jerked as though stung. 'Sim would never——'

'But Frank would! Did he mean to kill us?'

'Of course not!' she snapped.

'Sue!' Kent called.

'I'll say goodbye,' Mrs Colter said stiffly.

Sue held out her hand and the woman took it. She shook hands as a man does, quickly and firmly, and stood back. Kent came to the door and Sue left the house with him.

It was no use looking back, trying to memorise the house and surroundings. She knew that she would never forget it. She bent quickly and picked several violets as she passed. I'll press them, she thought. They'll be a memory of Undara, of the wide horizons, the desert trees and the hours

174

at Red Tors. Undara ... Long way. It had been a long way to come, and it would be too far for her to return to what she had been before.

On the trip she said little, but when they arrived at Yurla she waited until Nick had left them and asked Kent casually, 'Who was riding round the cattle the night of the stampede?'

'Frank,' Kent answered. 'Rory tore a strip off him the next day, I remember.'

Frank. She had known it before he spoke.

Sue found Sim seated in the Yurla kitchen. He was laughing and had a boy on each knee while he watched Marj's face as she sat and talked to him. The woman looked up, pleased. 'It's good to see you again, Miss Howard. How is your cold?'

Sue's momentary surprise died. They knew all that happened; it was like a village, and news travelled fast. 'I'm recovering,' she said, smiling.

The boys regarded her with solemn grey eyes and, when they spoke, they turned their faces so that Sim could see their mouths. They had been well and lovingly drilled to consider him. Sue did not linger and made an excuse to leave, knowing the circle there to be a complete and happy one. Nick was at the shed with Kent while they did some mechanical work on the car.

She did not want to go into the house, but she must enter her bedroom again and pack her things. Kent would run them to the airstrip.

He came through the garden with quick strides and his face lit up when he saw her. 'Ah, there you are, little lass. Where are you going?'

She turned from going to the waterhole. It was one of her memories of Rory and she could not walk there with Kent.

'Just looking at the garden,' she said lamely.

He fell into step beside her and put his arm through hers. 'We make a good team, Sue. Come to London with me?'

'I've just come from there.' She tried to keep her voice amused and light, but he refused to be put off.

'I'm a long way from success, Sue, but I'm determined to make it. I'm going to Mexico for my next trip. There are some wonderful subjects there and I have ideas for an exotic show——'

She let him outline his schemes and listened gravely. Dear Kent ... 'You'll do it,' she said sincerely, 'I know you will.'

'We'll do it together.'

She shook her head slowly, not wanting to hurt him, and he sighed. 'Isn't this the scenario where I get the girl?'

'Some day you will, Kent.'

'But not Sue, eh?' He grinned crookedly. 'The trouble is that I've neglected you. I should have concentrated on you more and worn you down.'

She smiled, 'You know that your work comes first.'

He admitted it wryly, absently noticing the contrast of her beautiful hair against the dark leaves of the tree behind her, and she knew the focus of his interest had shifted. One would not pin Kent for long. There would be a new challenge for him, a fresh angle on an old, familiar subject which would tease and tantalise his mind until he was able to express it and capture it in his work. Kent was lucky; he had a rewarding and absorbing interest which would not let him be too unhappy. He would find fulfilment in it and his loneliness could be forgotten.

Sue went to her room and began packing. Marj Settler came along the verandah and paused at the door.

'Are you leaving, Miss Howard?'

She sounded surprised and regretful and Sue called to

176

her to come in. 'My brother and I are returning to Brisbane, Marj.'

Marj's face was a study as she watched the younger girl. 'I wouldn't do that, Miss Howard. I wouldn't go just yet.'

Sue paused in the act of pushing her heavy jersey into an over-full bag. 'We—have our reasons, Marj.'

The woman smiled at her reprovingly. 'The Boss won't like it. He was very definite that you were to wait here until he returned.'

For another quarrel. For more pointless talk of Undara. 'We can't stay, Marj,' Sue said briefly.

'We're all at sixes and sevens here at the moment,' Marj confided. 'Sim and I hope to be married soon and will be living at Undara. His mother will take over my job here.'

'How do you get on with her, Marj?' asked Sue.

'We understand each other, Miss Howard, and she knows I'll care for Sim. We get on fine.'

'She's a personality,' Sue murmured.

'She's a battler. She's had it hard. She's a good woman when you get to know her well,' averred Marj.

'I didn't have the chance.'

Marj's eyebrows rose. 'She liked you, Sim told me. She said you were all right.'

Sue felt an absurd feeling of pleasure. 'I respect her, Marj.'

Marj grinned. 'Not like Miss Bedford, eh? A trouble-maker, that one! We were glad to see the back of her for a while.' Sue could not discuss Clare with her, and made a show of being busy. Marj opened the screen door, then paused. 'Did you hear that a message came over the transceiver that there's a camel drive on? The hunters are rounding up wild camels for a zoo.'

'Where are they working?' asked Sue.

'Somewhere at the back of Lake Frome. They sent

directions and I passed them on to Kent.'

Sue left her packing and walked over to the big shed. Kent was loading equipment aboard and his face was absorbed. Nick had an air of disappointment and protest about him, and greeted her disconsolately.

'Did you hear the news, Sue? Kent's off.'

Kent's smile was swift, but there was a hint of regret behind it. 'Down in the Lake Frome country, Sue.'

'Marj told me,' she said.

'I'm off as soon as I can be ready.'

Kent was cutting his losses. She felt her eyes sting, what use to cry out and beg him not to go? Their association was coming to an end and she must not make it difficult for him.

'We've—you've been marvellous to us, Kent. A true friend.' She faltered.

'You can say that again,' Nick put in.

He grinned at them both, the crooked grin she had grown to cherish.

'Come and help me carry, you two lazy Londoners. Marj and Sim are taking you out to the plane later.'

She understood. He did not want to be the one to stand and wave farewell. He drove to the gate in his car and they helped him pack his personal possessions. 'Don't fling them in like that!' Sue protested.

'All but the cameras,' he teased.

Sue kept her eyelids widely open, a trick which kept tears at bay.

'Sim's gone to the airstrip,' Kent announced.

She started. 'Should we have gone? Did he go without us?'

'You've another hour,' Kent comforted, 'the plane goes on to other stations and calls in on the way back.'

The inevitable moment came. He went in and said his

farewells to the staff and Sue waited with Nick beside the car. The kangaroo came and stood with them, his strangely horse-like face serious and intent as though he was aware of the emotions of the moment. Nick's hand caressed one of the animal's long ears as they waited.

'I'm going to miss it all,' he said simply and from his heart. 'I asked Kent to take me, Sue, but he wouldn't. He said my future doesn't lie with him.'

When Kent came back he walked quickly, as though he was determined there would be no delays. His handshake for Nick was sincere and he put his arms round Sue and hugged her warmly. 'Little Sue,' was all he said.

'Will we—see you again, Kent?' she asked tremulously.

He kissed her. 'Many times! I'll be in touch. Old Kent will be back, in and out of your lives! You'll see me, never fear.'

They stood back and watched the dust cloud rise and die behind the vehicle. Sue kept her head averted so that Nick could not see her face. If only she had been able to love Kent, how pleasant it could have been. Pleasant and happy ... there would have been none of the heady ecstasy which she knew, to her cost, love could bring.

They went in the gate to the homestead and she put on a brisk air to hide her feelings. 'You haven't packed. Come on, Nick. Time is getting away and Marj said she'll have a cup of tea ready for us before we go to the plane.'

In his bedroom she surveyed his clothing and remarked cautiously, 'You're an untidy devil, Nick. Mother ruined you.'

He looked around helplessly. 'I haven't much stuff with me.'

'Thank goodness for that! We'd never get in the door otherwise! Come on, start a-gatherin'.'

It's fortunate, she thought, that life gives us work in

times of stress. To be busy, to have one's hands occupied, does help . . .

Marj did not ring the bell but came to call them, and there was an odd air of excitement about her. 'Morning tea is in the dining room, Miss Howard.'

Sue thanked her and Nick carried his roll of bedding and his leather carry-all and dumped them on the path near the gate. The dining room was cool and shadowy after the brightness of the sunlit verandah, and Sue saw a man seated at the head of the table.

'Excuse me not rising,' he said.

The sudden shock made her stop, staring. She could not speak for a moment, but Nick entered and voiced their surprise and prevented a silence which could have betrayed her.

'Rory! How on earth did this happen?'

'Sheer nuisance value. The hospital was glad to be rid of me.' He put a hand to a walking stick beside his chair and nodded to the teapot. 'Would you pour, Sue, please?'

She drew a deep breath and steadied herself as she came forward. 'I'm glad to see you're recovering, Rory.'

He shrugged. 'I've been away from Yurla for too long as it is!'

Where was Clare? Sue was about to ask, but knew the other girl well enough to realise that she had gone to her room where she would rest from the trip and let Marj bring tea to her. For once Sue would pour the tea.

She lifted the silver pot and the freshly-baked scones were passed. Rory ate little and Sue, choking down her food, tried to hide her feelings. To see him again was a torture she had not expected. Her longing and love for him were emotions which she did not have under control, and it was difficult to sit at the same table and watch his drawn face and know there was nothing she could say, or do, to make herself part of his life.

180

He drained his cup and spoke directly to Nick. 'What I had in mind was this. Would you start here as jackeroo?'

Nick regarded him solemnly. 'What does it entail?'

'You live in the house, you learn to manage a property. I thought a year here, then time on other properties with other station owners so that you learn both sheep and cattle work. You have to get experience in what the bush is like and I warn you that I expect results! You must pull your weight.'

Sue saw that her brother was pleased and a look of delighted expectancy was on his face. 'Good grief, Rory! Do you mean——?'

'In time,' Rory explained patiently, 'you will run Undara. There will be no profit in it for you, or for me, but you can get another block of land on which to expand and rear your family, when you have one.'

'It'll take years.' Nick sounded undaunted.

Sue looked from one loved face to the other and felt excluded. Suddenly Nick had gone from her into a man's world; he had accepted a challenge which Rory presented in an unaccented, factual voice, offering no concessions, giving no promises of an easy path. Rory was right, Nick needed the firmness, needed responsibility.

He grinned at her. 'That sounds great, doesn't it, Sue?'

She agreed quietly and Nick blurted out, 'I'm sorry for the fool things I've said, Rory. That story about Uncle Dryden's death—the talk——'

Sue clasped her hands together under the table and watched Rory.

His eyes met hers. 'It was extraordinary how the wind of gossip swept that seed of doubt into the minds of men who knew Dryden. You see, he didn't die as he should have died. I'll tell you and we won't speak of it again.'

His voice was level. 'When he returned from hospital we realised—those of us who knew him best, Mrs Colter and

Sim, Frank and myself—that he was in more pain than he should have been. We said nothing. He was a proud man and we could only try to match his spirit. He was dying, and he knew it.' The bald story begged no mercy from them for his part in it. 'I spent as much time as I could with him. He had written to a sister-in-law before the accident, he told me, but wrote and cancelled his invitation to her when he was so badly disfigured. He didn't mention that she had any family, and I assumed that she was a widow and in moderate circumstances. He gave her no reason for changing his mind, I gathered, and perhaps his letter was a cold one.'

Sue realised why her mother had not told them of the invitation; she had been hurt and mortified when it had been recalled. Only in her last moments of consciousness had her thoughts returned to the letter, and the incomplete information she gave Sue had led them to take the long journey to this place, to this room, where they sat and listened to Rory's painful words.

'We kept him as happy and as comfortable as possible,' he added.

'Including his brandy?' Sue asked in a low voice.

Rory nodded. 'Why should he be denied? He willed Undara to me so that I could carry out his scheme for it and preserve the wildlife and the aboriginal relics.'

He moved uneasily in his chair. 'One afternoon when I was at Undara he asked me to go with Sim to check some work on a distant fence. While we were away he ordered Frank to saddle his horse, the black stallion. Mrs Colter protested, evidently, but at last helped him to dress. Frank pulled on his boots and they supported him to the horse yards——'

The autumn sun streamed on to the floor of the verandah and bird calls sounded from the garden. The curtains moved slightly in the breeze at the door.

'They knew what he intended to do,' he said slowly. 'When Sim and I came back they were at the yards. They were waiting there. They realised what the extra weeks of life would mean for him—pain, hospitalisation, exile from Undara.'

Sue remembered Frank's bitterness when speaking of the city. 'Too hard and cruel' ... She knew how deep had been his loyalty to his 'mate'.

'So they let him ride.' Rory put it in few words.

Sue's throat was tight. She could see it clearly. The emaciated, determined man and the quiet, stricken people who loved him and watched him ride away.

'He left a message that the horse must not be blamed. The stallion is powerful and was wild and half-broken at the time,' Rory said. 'We found Dryden when the sun went down, on the dry lake bed beyond the red sandhill. He'd been thrown from the saddle.'

Nick was silenced and Sue spoke reflectively. 'Outsiders didn't know that he was ill. Is that why bushmen speculated——?'

Rory nodded. 'He was a good rough rider and wouldn't have been thrown if he had had his strength. Then I inherited the place!' His smile was tinged with bitterness. 'I let the whispers pass. I knew they'd realise in time what the plans were for Undara and conjecture would be finished.'

'Then we arrived and stirred things up,' Nick looked regretful. 'Why the dickens didn't you flatten me straight away?'

Rory laughed. 'You deserved it! You couldn't have arrived at a worse time. The busy period, Clare here—I had little time to clear up the complex situation of Undara, and didn't know if I could trust you with Dryden's secret.'

Nick's eyes, so like his mother's, were serene. 'What do we do now?'

'You go and unpack your stuff. Mrs East has sent your

heavier luggage by road transport and Sim has placed it in your room. Sort it out. Tidily! An untidy man runs an untidy property!' He gestured to the door. 'Out! I want to talk to your sister.'

Sue felt desolate as Nick left, without a backward glance. So she was alone! She felt a spasm of self-pity and forced it back. She had wanted security for Nick and he would have it now.

Rory put his hand out to her. 'Give me a heave up, will you? We'll go into the sitting room.' He got to his feet slowly and said with annoyance, 'I'll be glad to fling this stick aside!'

The tone was so typical of him that she had to laugh. 'You'll do as the doctor tells you, I hope!'

'It won't take me long to recover,' he said firmly.

He sat on the couch and she stood apart from him, keeping her hands in the pocket of her jacket.

'Sit down!' he said forcefully. 'There are a couple more things to be cleared up. I felt it unnecessary to tell Nick. It's about Clare——'

She seated herself and pushed her hair back from her face. It was best to look into the fireplace where the fire was laid ready for evening, and not into his watchful eyes. 'Is—she all right?' she asked.

'Clare is always all right,' he said crisply. 'This is a confession, really. She tells me she took the jerrycans out of the car the day you drove to Undara.'

She was distressed for him and said breathlessly, 'As if it matters now! She'd be joking, playing a trick on me—she wouldn't realise——'

He watched her. 'No, she wouldn't realise that it could have been a very serious matter. Her reason for doing it was an odd one; she felt jealous, it seems. She felt that I was getting a little too interested in you.'

Sue said hurriedly, 'How—foolish of her! I'm sorry we caused so much trouble.' She jumped to her feet and went to stand on the hearth. 'I'm going today. Things will settle down between you, Rory.'

'Do you think so?' he asked wearily. 'You know she let the search for us go on in the opposite direction from the one we had taken? I told her distinctly that we were going to Red Tors. She was hitting back at us for going together!'

It was the greatest test of Sue's life. The happiness of his marriage depended on his trust in Clare, and she would not undermine it. She stood very straight and forced herself to laugh. 'Goodness! It would be an accident! She must have felt awful when she knew of her mistake. The names are all new to her——'

'I accept that,' he agreed.

'She's had a tough spin, I think,' Sue added reflectively. 'From what she says about her parents——'

'Her mother is a gentle, sweet-natured woman,' he said, and fiddled with his walking stick. 'She's torn between Clare's father and Clare. She's a quiet woman.'

'Oh.' Sue digested the information, surprised. 'One gained an impression——'

'That her mother was mean? She has little money. Clare's father gives her nothing, and she's undemanding. Clare is more like her father.'

She felt empty and drained with the effort of keeping her face guarded and her expression one of friendly interest. She could bear no more. 'It must be time I left for the airstrip.'

Rory stiffened. 'Must you go, Sue? I saw Kent on his way out past the strip and he tells me that he's no more than a friend to you.' He held out his hand, offering more

185

than a gesture. 'Clare has gone, Sue. Kent told me that he'd passed that news on to you.'

She recalled Kent sitting beside her in the bedroom at Undara and telling her that Clare had gone in the plane, and she stared at him. 'I thought she'd gone to town to be with you when you were in hospital.'

'She got the search organised in the wrong direction, and when Gerry Darker came she left Undara and went to Sydney with him,' he said.

'Oh, Rory, I'm sorry! She shouldn't have——! Was it because of me? Let me explain to her——'

'Explain that there was nothing between us?' His teasing air made her feel stupid.

'Exactly,' she said breathlessly.

'Isn't there?' he asked. His eyes had narrowed as he watched her and she felt the blood drain from her heart.

'Rory!'

'She knew.' His voice was deep and compelling. 'She knew I was drawn to you, Sue, the first time you walked on to the verandah here at Yurla. You were so right for me and the house seemed to welcome you.'

'But you were engaged,' she said.

He shook his head. 'No. I was brought up to believe, however, that a gentleman doesn't set a lady down in public! Clare and I had a brief attachment when she was out here with her mother, who's a friend of Essie East's, for the Picnic Races. I invited Mrs Bedford up for the festivities because she came from the district as a girl and had a lot of old friends. Clare came with her.'

'Clare was sure you were——'

'She made it clear from the start that I was part of her plans for the future. Then she seemed to have second thoughts and went overseas to her father, and I thought she would soon forget.'

Sue heard a clock chime somewhere in the house, but it was very quiet when Rory spoke again. 'Then she cabled that she was returning and coming to Yurla. I went to meet her, determined to have a clear-cut arrangement with her before we left the city: she was welcome as a friend. We had to be clear on that!'

'You let Kent bring her,' she pointed out.

He grinned wickedly. 'I know how Kent travels! I know he forgets the comfort of his passengers when he gets wrapped up in his photography!'

'You did it on purpose!'

'Not altogether,' he admitted. 'I had to return immediately and that was that! The evening she arrived here we had a frank talk and I told her we were friends, no more.'

Sue recalled Clare's determined talk of what she would do when she was mistress at Yurla, and knew that the girl's twisted determination had brooked no denial. 'You gave her a taste of hard living,' she chided, 'dragging her out on the muster—the early hours—the discomforts!'

'It's part of my life,' he pointed out. Then he said commandingly, 'If you don't come and sit down beside me I shall have to come over there and fetch you!'

She sank to the cushions at his side and he put his arms about her. She had dreamed of his kisses, but his mouth was harder and more passionate than she had imagined. How could she have thought him undemonstrative?

'Does that convince you?' he asked briskly.

Her open, shining love was in her face for him to see. 'Was I meant to die when Clare let me go off without water?'

'As if I would leave you there!' he flashed. 'I've had a bad time, Sue, aware of Mrs Colter's and Frank's foolish and dangerous attempts to scare you off. They took their vow to Dryden seriously, and saw you as a threat to his

187

plans. As for Clare—she wrote me a bitter, spiteful letter when she left Undara. I've destroyed it. She's her father's daughter, and she'll seek what's best for herself at all times.'

'She must have suffered,' Sue said. 'I'm sorry she was jealous of me, Rory.'

'If she was jealous I know how she felt.' He held her close. 'How I resented good old Kent at times! As for Gerry——'

She laughed, 'To think that I didn't know!'

'My feelings for Clare had been very shallow,' he confessed. 'I looked for something deep and lasting in my marriage. Something like the love Dryden had kept alive in his heart for so long. He loved his Nora until the day he died.'

Sue lifted her face to his. 'My mother!'

He spoke reflectively. 'Dryden was my father's friend originally and I looked up to him and admired him when I was a lad. Dad told me once that Dryden had come to Australia because the girl he loved had married another man.'

'His half-brother,' Sue whispered.

'The one man he couldn't fight for her! They must have been close when they were young, the two men?'

'I believe so,' she agreed.

He bent his head and kissed her again. 'You like Yurla, don't you, Sue?'

'I love it,' she said fervently.

He traced the line of her cheek with a tender touch.

'Don't blame yourself for Uncle Dryden's death,' she whispered.

'I could have stopped it because I'd sensed his decision, but I shall never regret that I didn't interfere. I'm only sorry that it had repercussions that hurt you.'

'We haven't been hurt,' she responded, 'we came for adventure and—heavens! Have we had it!'

She heard him make a wheezing noise and, startled, found he was laughing and trying to stifle it, grimacing as he did so.

'You're a brave little girl, aren't you? Will you marry me, Sue? You know and share my interests, and I love you. Is Yurla too far out and remote a place for you?'

'This is home now, Rory,' she said sincerely, 'this, and Undara. Our journey wasn't a long way, after all.'

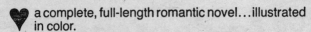

In every issue...

Here's what you'll find:

♥ a complete, full-length romantic novel...illustrated in color.

♥ exotic travel feature...an adventurous visit to a romantic faraway corner of the world.

♥ delightful recipes from around the world...to bring delectable new ideas to your table.

♥ reader's page...your chance to exchange news and views with other Harlequin readers.

♥ other features on a wide variety of interesting subjects.

Start enjoying your own copies of Harlequin magazine immediately by completing the subscription reservation form.

Not sold in stores!